AGE DOESN'T MATTER IN POOL

What matters is playing smart.

My dad was a world-class player. I've seen him play on videos my mom took when he was on the professional nine-ball circuit. He was big—six feet two inches—and when he leaned over a pool table, he'd smile and shoot his stick fast like a rifle. On a video Mom took in Atlantic City he ran 289 balls without missing. He had jet-black hair and brown eyes. His favorite color was blue. I've got everything about him memorized good.

He would have become nine-ball champion of the world if he hadn't gotten all that cancer.

He died when I was eight months old.

That leaves me to be nine-ball champion of the world someday.

But first I've got to beat Buck.

Books by
JOAN BAUER

STICKS

JOAN BAUER

STICKS

speak
An Imprint of Penguin Group (USA) Inc.

SPEAK
Published by the Penguin Group
Penguin Group (USA) Inc., 345 Hudson Street, New York, New York 10014, U.S.A.
Penguin Group (Canada), 10 Alcorn Avenue, Toronto, Ontario, Canada M4V 3B2
(a division of Pearson Penguin Canada Inc.)
Penguin Books Ltd, 80 Strand, London WC2R 0RL, England
Penguin Ireland, 25 St Stephen's Green, Dublin 2, Ireland
(a division of Penguin Books Ltd)
Penguin Group (Australia), 250 Camberwell Road, Camberwell, Victoria 3124, Australia
(a division of Pearson Australia Group Pty Ltd)
Penguin Books India Pvt Ltd, 11 Community Centre,
Panchsheel Park, New Delhi - 110 017, India
Penguin Group (NZ), Cnr Airborne and Rosedale Roads, Albany,
Auckland, New Zealand (a division of Pearson New Zealand Ltd)
Penguin Books (South Africa) (Pty) Ltd, 24 Sturdee Avenue,
Rosebank, Johannesburg 2196, South Africa

Registered Offices: Penguin Books Ltd, 80 Strand, London WC2R 0RL, England

First published in the United States of America by Delacorte Press, 1996
Published simultaneously by G. P. Putnam's Sons and Puffin Books,
divisions of Penguin Putnam Books for Young Readers, 2002
This edition published by Speak, an imprint of Penguin Group (USA) Inc., 2005

1 3 5 7 9 10 8 6 4 2

THE LIBRARY OF CONGRESS HAS CATALOGED THE G. P. PUTNAM'S SONS EDITION AS FOLLOWS:
Bauer, Joan, date.
Sticks / Joan Bauer.—1st G. P. Putnam's Sons ed.
p. cm.
Summary: With the help of his grandmother, his dead father's best friend, and his
own best friend, a math genius, ten-year-old Mickey prepares to compete in the
most important pool championship of his life, despite his mother's reservations.
ISBN 0-399-23752-6
[1. Pool (Game)—Fiction. 2. Mothers and sons—Fiction. 3. Fathers and sons—Fiction.
4. Grandmothers—Fiction. 5. Friendship—Fiction. 6. Mathematics—Fiction.] I. Title.
PZ7.B32615St 2002   [Fic]—dc21   2001018597

Speak ISBN 0-14-240428-4

Printed in the United States of America

Once again, for Evan

STICKS

Wham.

Buck Pender rams the five ball into the side pocket and leans across the pool table like a gorilla.

"Just keeps getting worse, don't it?" he says like I'm supposed to say, "Yeah, Buck, I quit. I just can't take it. You're the greatest."

Buck tips the six ball into the side pocket and gives me his fat smile. The bearded guy on table eight is watching me. I hold my stick tough like I don't care that I'm getting crushed by an ape-boy in my own family's pool hall.

Buck misses an easy bank shot on the seven and steps back like I'm diseased. Here's the thing about nine ball: Whoever gets the nine in on a legal shot wins—it doesn't matter if every other ball you hit goes in perfect. The nine ball is king.

I study the table for the best shot as Arlen Pepper eats a Raisinet. Arlen is my best friend. Sometimes he's my coach too. Some people say he doesn't look old enough to be in fifth grade—he's short and skinny with a bunch of blond hair that never stays put.

He wipes off his glasses and studies the table. We've worked out signals between us like pitchers and catchers use in the heat of a big game. Arlen taps his new Red Sox cap and coughs twice, which means I should go for the bank shot—that's when you bounce a ball off the rail and into a pocket. Bank shots are my specialty because I'm good at math. Pool is pure geometry, plus a little physics.

Pow.

I bank the seven ball at a ninety-degree angle and watch it zip into the corner. Arlen shakes his box of Raisinets, which means good shot.

"Lucky," Buck says, hissing.

I nail the eight in the side. Tell me about lucky.

I do a little dance around the table to show I'm hot. I chalk my stick light—losers chalk hard. Only the nine ball's left. If I make it, I get some pride back. Buck's beating me five games to zip. There's nobody I want to beat worse than him.

My hands are sweating. That's death to a pool player—sweaty hands make your stick slip. I wipe them on my jeans. I stretch to reach the white cue ball.

I'm thinking about Buck's fat face.

Thinking about all the times he's pushed me around.

Arlen's tapping and coughing hard; he wants me to bank the nine. It's a maniac shot off two rails. I look up at him. *I can't make that shot!*

I aim my stick for a big slice on the nine instead. The sweat keeps coming. Arlen's tugging at his earlobe, which means I'm making a mistake. I hit the white cue ball just as my stick slips. The nine ball misses the pocket.

"Ahhh!" I ram my stick on the floor.

Buck goes, "Tsk, tsk." He rams the nine in the side. I close my eyes and hear it roll inside the table.

"Game, *Vernon.*"

Buck kisses his stick and walks off laughing. He stops at the red shirt with the white lettering that's hanging in the big window that faces Flax Street, the main drag in town. I don't like him near that shirt. It reads:

VERNON'S POOL HALL
YOUTH TOURNAMENT CHAMPION
CRUCKSTON, NEW JERSEY

The tournament's for ten- to thirteen-year-olds and I'm finally old enough to compete. Pool is big stuff in this town. Vernon's makes sure of it. We've got special deals for kids and families, free lessons on Saturdays. When the paper mill on Grossmont Street closed down, Poppy, my grandmother, let all those out-of-work folks and their families play pool for free on Wednesday afternoons for a whole year. We got a plaque from the mayor saying how for forty years Vernon's has been an anchor for the town. Poppy keeps it on the shelf above the cash register next to her bottle of Pepto-Bismol.

Buck's not looking at the plaque. He turns to me with his thirteen-year-old's sneer: "The shirt's mine,

Vernon!" and walks out the door like God's gift to the galaxy.

"You're not winning it!" Arlen screams after him. "Mickey's going to win it because you're a stupid moron!"

The bearded guy on table eight is watching me again like he's trying to figure something out. I don't like being watched when I've lost. I look at the gray tile floor. I look at the old paneled walls. I feel the roll of the green cloth on table seven. We've got twenty-four Brunswick pool tables at Vernon's and I've played on every one.

Now it might sound impossible, me, a ten-year-old, gunning to beat a teenager, but I can beat lots of kids my age and older in this hall. I've got pool in my blood.

I'm tall for my age—five-four to be exact. This puts me dead even with Poppy except when she stands on her toes to holler. I've got long arms and big hands like my dad, light brown hair like my mom.

My grandparents built this hall forty years ago and stuck their house on top of it because Grandpa didn't want anything between him and the tables. It's a big house, too, the only one in the business district—every inch of it brick-laid, like the hall below, with eight long rooms and a secret passageway going up to the roof. The roof's so cool; being on top of things makes you feel important. It's got a black iron fence around it so no one can fall off.

I had my tenth birthday party up there last September. Guys came up the passageway, which you get to through my closet; it was dark like always be-

4

cause the light doesn't work. We took flashlights and made it up the creaky stairs. I had everybody feel raw egg in a bowl and told them it was a brain. We could see the old abandoned paper mill and the blinking LOANS WHILE U WAIT sign and the big trucks rolling six blocks away on the New Jersey Turnpike. Then me, Arlen, Petie Pencastle, T. R. Dobbs, and Reed Jaworski slept in a tent even though it was raining. It was the best party I ever had.

My dad learned to shoot in this very hall. I did too. Dad was beating adults when he was twelve years old. Like my grandmother Poppy says—age doesn't matter in pool. What matters is playing smart. My dad was a world-class player. I've seen him play on videos my mom took when he was on the professional nine-ball circuit. He was big—six feet two inches—and when he leaned over a pool table, he'd smile and shoot his stick fast like a rifle. On a video Mom took in Atlantic City he ran 289 balls without missing. He had jet-black hair and brown eyes. His favorite color was blue. I've got everything about him memorized good.

He would have become nine-ball champion of the world if he hadn't gotten all that cancer.

He died when I was eight months old.

That leaves me to be nine-ball champion of the world someday.

But first I've got to beat Buck.

Arlen's staring at me. He's mad I didn't try to bank the nine ball.

"You forgot your secret weapon?" Arlen yells. "You forgot *math*?"

"I didn't forget."

5

I didn't know anything about the connection between math and pool until Arlen pointed it out to me two years ago when we were in third grade. I was standing on an A&W crate practicing bank shots when Arlen leaped up all excited and told me I was doing geometry. I'd heard of geometry. I just didn't know what it was.

"It's about measurements," Arlen said, "and how points, lines, and angles go together. I'm studying it with Mr. Blodgett!"

Now, I'd grown up in a pool hall and no one had ever mentioned geometry to me. But Arlen had been in gifted math programs since he was in first grade, so I figured I was getting the inside track. Arlen pointed at the eight ball lying close to the rail of the table. "How are you going to shoot that, Mickey?"

"I'm going to hit it hard and hope it bounces into the corner."

"But why are you going to do that?"

I look around. "Because this is a pool hall and I'm not playing checkers."

"But *why* does it work?"

I was about to say it works because that's how you play pool.

"It *works*," said Arlen, "because bank shots use geometric angles. When you hit the eight ball at a certain angle to the rail, it will bounce off the rail at the same angle."

Arlen called it the angle of incidence always equaling the angle of reflection. He took out a notepad and drew this picture. I saved it for studying.

"So when you make a bank shot, you're using geometry to do it!" Arlen sat back like he'd just invented chocolate.

We drew a lot more diagrams and I kept trying shots and measuring the angles. After a few weeks, my bank shots were better. After a few months, my whole game was cleaner.

Arlen won't let me forget it. Like now.

"Math," he's shouting, waving his protractor, which he takes everywhere, "will never fail you! You think Buck's got a secret weapon?"

"Skill," I say.

"That's not a winning attitude!"

The bearded man on table eight makes an unbelievable triple bank and runs the rest of the balls like an absolute ace. I rub the Band-Aids covering the blisters I've got on both hands from practicing so hard. The guy puts down his stick and says, "Listen, son, you could have won that game."

Is he kidding? If I could have won, I would have.

The man racks the balls on table eight, pulls back his right arm, and *pow* like a rifle, three balls go in on the break. He picks the rest of the balls off like nothing, piles them in the rack, slaps a cowboy hat on his head, and tucks his thumb in his fat leather belt, which has a silver buckle shaped like a wild horse.

"I'd watch that focus of yours, son," the man says. "You're missing more shots than you need to."

What's he talking about?

The man looks over at Poppy, who's dusting her Hall of Fame photographs of the pool greats of the world, which line the wall by the odd-numbered tables. She's giving Allen Hopkins, Willie Mosconi, and Machine Gun Lou Butera an extra go with the cloth. Poppy takes everything about pool serious. When Hanrahan's House of Pool opened across town with its cheap tables, bad sticks, and discount coupons, Poppy stuck a poster in our window:

> REAL POOL.
> ALWAYS HAD IT.
> ALWAYS WILL.

Hanrahan's closed in two years. Poppy says there's no substituting for quality.

Poppy's wearing her gray Vernon's sweatshirt. She wears one every day, except in the summer and for church on Sunday. She sells them behind the counter—red, blue, and gray; VERNON'S is spelled out big on the front and back so people can see where you've been whether you're coming or going.

Poppy's run Vernon's ever since Grandpa died (which was long before I was born), even though everyone told her it was no job for a woman. She's kept it like Grandpa would have, too, except for the time three years ago when she put in the snack bar and had to take it out because guys were getting Cheez Whiz on the tables. We've got vending machines in the back now by the storage closet.

Poppy raises her dustcloth and smacks a fly dead that landed on her sign:

THIS IS VERNON'S—
IF YOU SPIT, YOU'RE OUT
IF YOU SWEAR, YOU'RE OUT.
IF YOU'RE TROUBLE, DON'T COME IN.
—EDWINA P. VERNON, PROPRIETRESS

The man with the beard laughs a little when she does it. "Well . . . ," he says, drawing the word out slow, "I'd best be going."

He walks to the counter to turn in his rack. He stands there a minute, looking at the pool trophies

my dad won lining the shelves of the glass case behind the counter.

NEW JERSEY STATE 9 BALL CHAMPION
U.S. TOURNAMENT OF CHAMPIONS
PEPSI OPEN CHAMPION
RAK M UP CLASSIC CHAMPION
ROCKY MOUNTAIN OPEN CHAMPION

Poppy and my mom have fights sometimes about
whether the trophies should stay up or get put
away. Poppy says if Mom wants them down, she'll
do it, and Mom says she can't make the decision
herself. I can't imagine that case without Dad being
part of it.

The man puts his money down and tips his hat to
Poppy, who watches him strange and keeps on
watching as he walks out of the hall through the big
oak door like a sheriff going to clean up a town.

Arlen and I turn like one kid and head out the
door too, just as the man crosses Flax Street. He
walks straight and fast, past Mrs. Cassetti's bakery
and the big wedding cake she keeps in the window;
past the fix-it shop, where Mr. Kopchnik sits outside
in his chair, taking apart a blender, listening to op-
era; past Crystal's Launderette, where he opens the
door for Mrs. Merman and her granddaughter Sa-
mantha, who's carrying the laundry basket. Then
he climbs into the cab of a huge green truck.

The April wind picks up.

The man revs the engine.

It's the shiniest truck I've ever seen: a Peterbilt—
the ultimate. He pulls her out easy—the truck's

shining like an emerald—and moves down Flax Street past the old gray buildings and boarded-up stores, leaving thunder in his path.

Arlen and I stand there feeling the rumble.

"Who was that guy?" we whisper.

The whole next day, I wonder if I really could have won that game.

I think about it during music appreciation class and get in trouble when Ms. Weisenberg, in that singing voice of hers, asks me who is the youngest classical composer of all time and I say Minnesota Fats.

I think about it during gym and mess up guarding the soccer goal and don't even notice when T.R. kicks the ball right past me into the net. Coach Crow blows his whistle loud and asks me if I enjoyed my nap.

I think about it when Mrs. Riggles, everybody's favorite teacher at Grover Cleveland Elementary School, floats a plastic boat stuffed with Lipton tea bags in a tub of water and starts throwing the tea off the boat, angry, like they did at the Boston Tea

Party. I stop thinking about it then because things are getting interesting.

Mrs. Riggles shakes back her long black hair, puts a hand on her pregnant stomach, and says, "Okay, colonists, get mad!"

The class starts shouting how we've had it with the British and we're sick of being taxed. T. R. Dobbs and Petie Pencastle yell about being free; Sally Costner screams she isn't going to take it anymore. Arlen gets up on a chair and cries that no ships bringing tea from England will be allowed to land in our ports. We all shout, "Yeah!" and Mrs. Riggles throws the last tea bag in the tub as the water turns brown.

We just started studying the American Revolution. We've been decorating our room with maps we made of the thirteen colonies. We wrote down famous quotes like Patrick Henry's, "Give me liberty or give me death," and hung them from the ceiling with string. History is my favorite subject. Mrs. Riggles says to understand where we're going we've got to know where we've been.

It's three-thirty. Arlen and I are walking the eight blocks from school to his house. We only take the school bus when the weather's bad; the bus fumes make Arlen carsick. A blast of wind shoots down Mariah Boulevard and rattles a trash can. Arlen stops dead in front of Suds' Diner and looks at his reflection in the window with the cartoon drawing of a bathtub with suds flowing out of it. He starts

13

feeling behind his back. He's lost his bookbag again —the fourth time in two weeks.

"My father," he shouts, "is going to *explode.* You're supposed to help me remember!"

"I forgot."

"I'm the one who forgets stuff," Arlen screams, "not you! I'll never get my tree house built!"

Arlen wants a tree house almost as much as I want to cream Buck. His parents are using this to solve his problem: forgetting his bookbag, forgetting his hat, forgetting his coat, boots, gloves, and sweaters all over town. If Arlen remembers to bring everything home for a week, his parents work on the tree house for an hour on Saturday. If he forgets, even once in a week, nothing happens. Silence.

There's been a lot of silence this month.

"Do you think that cowboy was right yesterday?" I ask him. "Do you think I could have won that game?"

A whiff of frying onions comes from Suds' as Arlen's shoulders slump. "There's not enough data to give an informed opinion."

"I don't think I'm missing more shots than I need to!"

Arlen shakes his head and moves slowly toward home. "Don't worry about something you can't prove, Mickey. Let's worry about something *factual* —like how my father is going to kill me!"

All the lights are out again in Arlen Pepper's kitchen. His mother is standing on a ladder holding a drill. Another blown fuse.

Arlen fiddles with his Red Sox cap and listens. "The stereo is on, the TV is off, no air-conditioning." He's adding the watts of the stuff plugged into each circuit breaker and dividing by the volts to solve the problem. "Too many amps for the kitchen circuit breaker, Mom."

"I forgot about the stereo."

Mrs. Pepper climbs down the ladder fast with one hand on her carpenter's belt. She steps over the pile of cabinet doors on the floor, hops over paint cans. Mr. and Mrs. Pepper own Pepper Construction Company, so their house always looks like a construction site. Mrs. Pepper is the tallest mother in the fifth grade and Mr. Pepper is the shortest father. Arlen used to measure them when he was younger; he kept a wall chart to see if his father had grown. Mrs. Pepper stayed at five-eleven. Mr. Pepper never moved past five-five.

Arlen is the math whiz of the entire fifth grade. Put a pool cue in his hands and he falls apart. Arlen says that with math it's absolutely certain that when you finish a problem, you have an answer. Grownups can tell you all sorts of things that you might find out later are wrong, but if they tell you there are only a hundred square yards of grass on a football field, all it takes is a pencil and a piece of paper to prove them wrong. So many things don't work without math—that's why it's the language of science. Arlen and I are doing a demonstration project for the science fair on the mathematics and physics of shooting pool and we're going to win first prize—unless Rory Magellan comes up with something better.

Rory is nine years old and only in fourth grade, but he's already got an award from the *Mr. Science* TV show for the photographs he sent in showing the weather station he built in his tree house. Mr. Science called him "a young scientist to watch" right on the show. This really killed Arlen because Mr. Science is Arlen's only hero who's still alive—Albert Einstein and Galileo are dead. It doesn't help that Rory has a tree house.

Arlen scribbles a note about his lost bookbag—I'M TOO YOUNG TO DIE—and puts it on his father's chair. The TOO YOUNG is underlined three times.

"He'll see it when he gets home from work," Arlen says. "Maybe he'll be merciful."

We head outside with Mangler, Arlen's black-and-white pet potbellied pig. "Jump," Arlen says, and Mangler jumps right over a small piece of pipe in the backyard. "Good pig," Arlen says as Mangler snorts. Mangler is a miniature pig and only weighs sixty-one pounds. He's the coolest animal in New Jersey.

Arlen sits at the base of the oak tree where his tree house is slowly getting built and touches the sign he made with his wood-burning kit to scare off bad guys.

```
BEWARE
ATTACK PIG ON PREMISES
ENTER AT YOUR OWN RISK
THIS MEANS YOU
I'M NOT KIDDING
```

Mangler likes the sign. He rears back his head and makes his loud squeal like something from beyond the grave. Not everyone knows this is typical pig behavior. Once Arlen and I were walking him on his leash when these older boys started shoving us around, going "Piggy, piggy" at Mangler. This is never a good idea because Mangler's real sensitive.

Arlen said to them, "I'll warn you now, this pig is a killer."

"Oh yeah?" the head boy said. "You think I'm scared of some *piggy?*"

"He's a total destruction machine," Arlen said, and gave Mangler's leash a little pull, which is Mangler's signal to become Super Mutant Avenger Pig —snorting and squealing and showing his pig teeth. This doesn't sound like much, but an irritated pig isn't pretty.

The boys jumped back.

"You let us pass," Arlen said, "or I'll let him go!"

Mangler was squealing like a killer beast from the crypt. The boys tore off and we were saved. Arlen is the second-shortest boy in the whole fifth grade, but with a maniac pig and attitude he does okay.

I asked Poppy once if Mangler could hang around Vernon's to spook Buck. She said she had enough animals in the hall already. "If you're expecting a pig to save you, Mickey Vernon, you'd better think again. Making you miserable is just what Buck Pender is aiming to do."

"It's not fair!"

"It's sure not." Poppy whacked the cash register drawer, which gets stuck when it rains. "You're expecting life to be fair, you're in for one raw disappointment."

Arlen's looking up at his hardly built tree house and shakes his head. Half the base is laid around the tree's fat branches, the ladder's up, but that's it. Mostly, Arlen's tree house is pieces of wood on the ground, covered by a tarp. In the beginning, we figured his parents couldn't keep up the torture, but Mr. and Mrs. Pepper are strong people. Now it seems that there's nothing left for Arlen to do but change.

Arlen throws a stick. "Life's not fair."

"No kidding."

"Parents just concentrate on the thing that drives them nuts and all the other good stuff you do goes out the window."

"Please, God. Please, God."

It's an hour later. Arlen's racing down Delby Street. I'm right behind him. Arlen remembered that he left his bookbag outside Vinnie's Variety when he retied his shoelace on the way home from school and we need to get it back before his father comes home. We rip past the old, gray Woolworth's. Gray is a big color in Cruckston, New Jersey. Poppy says the old paper mill shot up so much pollution when it was operating that it covered the town with a gray mist. People get around that by painting their front doors bright colors. Arlen's door is yellow; Vernon's door is pool table green. We tear across Mariah Boulevard, past a guy who's scratching his red beard, scratching his torn sweater, hanging on to a lamppost—drunk. He crashes into the street, right in front of a bus, which screeches to a stop, missing him. I watch to make sure he gets across the street okay.

"Oh, look!" says bad news stepping from the alley. "It's *Vernon!*"

My heart sinks. Buck Pender shoves me with his shoulder and pushes me toward the alley.

"Stop it!" I say.

Buck's blocking our way with Freddie Castle and Pike Lorey. They're so big it's like a wall went up in front of us. Pike takes a long drag on his cigarette and throws it on the ground. Freddie spits out a wad from his fat mouth. Buck smiles ugly. "Who's going to make me, *Vernon?*"

He always says my name like I don't deserve to have it. I want to hurt him so bad for all the times he's pushed me around and humiliated me at pool and—

"Leave him alone!" Arlen shouts.

"You talking to me?" Buck rubs his flat nose and struts toward Arlen. "How'd you like to have your face rearranged, squirt?"

Arlen gulps big.

Freddie and Pike step forward in their leather jackets and clench their dirty fists.

We sure could use Mangler now. I'm wondering if it's better to get beat up with your eyes opened or closed.

Suddenly a rumble shakes the street. The big green Peterbilt truck roars up and pulls to a stop. The guy with the beard shouts, "Those punks bothering you?"

19

"Yes!" Arlen shrieks. "*Yes!* They've been bothering us all our lives!"

The man jumps out of the truck. *"Back off!"* he yells at Buck and his ghouls, who race off around the corner.

"You boys okay?"

We nod, catching our breath.

He watches us to make sure. "I don't tolerate bullies." He scrapes his cowboy boot on the curb.

"That's good," says Arlen.

He points a long finger at us. "Those punks bother you again, you tell 'em you've got friends."

"Yeah," we say, grinning.

"All right then."

He stands there for a minute like he's got more to say, then he climbs back in the Peterbilt. It's got chrome around the doors and giant killer wheels. On the door is a painted horse—dark brown and white with a thrown-back head and energy coming out of it like it's alive. I step on the runner to shake the guy's hand, firm, like Poppy taught me.

"Thanks, mister!"

He reaches down and shakes back firm like me.

He rams the Peterbilt in gear. "Move 'em out, boys!"

I jump off the runner and step back as the great truck blasts off, shaking the potholes on Mariah Boulevard.

CHAPTER

Arlen gets his bookbag back, but forgets about the I'M TOO YOUNG TO DIE note on his father's chair. His dad says leaving the bookbag at Vinnie's *counts*. It doesn't matter that we almost got beaten to a pulp getting it back and would have died if we hadn't gotten saved by that awesome cowboy driving the biggest truck in America.

I'm waiting to tell my mom about it. Mom's sitting at her rolltop desk in her bedroom talking on the phone, trying to convince Mrs. Looper to join the citizens' crime patrol that she helped set up two years ago when all those burglaries started happening in Cruckston.

"Lyla," Mom says into the phone, "we've got formal rules from the police. We never get out of the car, we never chase anyone, we never apprehend or question. If anything looks suspicious, we call 911."

Mom takes off her reading glasses, which are held

together by a safety pin, and smiles tired. She's an assistant nursery-school teacher during the day, goes to college three nights a week to get her teaching degree, and helps run the crime patrol when she's not sleeping. Mom picks up a yellow sheet from the stack on her bed that reads A TOWN IS WATCHING, and tells Mrs. Looper about the training session next month for new volunteers. Mom hangs up the phone and shakes her head.

"If people just understood that it only takes a few hours once or twice a month to make a difference." Mom checks off Mrs. Looper's name on her weekly call sheet.

I nod and yank her thick brown ponytail to make her smile. When Mom smiles, her freckles light up. I say she should send the citizens' patrol to Buck Pender's apartment and drag him out in handcuffs.

"What happened?"

I tell her about Buck and the cowboy. It takes a few minutes to convince her I'm okay. She scrunches up the A TOWN IS WATCHING sheet and throws it on the blue rug. Then she puts her arm around my shoulder and we go into the kitchen. "A cowboy in Cruckston, New Jersey," she says. "Now that's something I'd like to see."

I sit at the counter on the wobbly white stool and start peeling potatoes for dinner. I help with dinner three nights a week; Mom says she's got a responsibility to the world to raise a male who can cook. I'm concentrating on getting the potatoes perfect, digging the peeler into the brown spots. Mom's skinning chicken pieces.

"What do you think Dad would be like if he was still alive?" I ask her.

She puts her knife down and looks out the kitchen window. "He'd still be very handsome."

I groan.

She's looking at a chicken leg now, smiling sad. "He would have won a lot more championship titles by now, I think."

"We'd be rich, I bet!"

"I imagine he'd be working on old cars, still, honey, trying to get them going. We'd probably have six of them in the alley in various stages of disrepair."

"I bet he could teach me how to beat Buck."

"He would have given it one huge try." She squeezes my hand. "He'd be so proud of you and your sister. . . ."

I swallow hard. "He'd be proud of all of us."

"Yes he would. We're doing all right around here."

Mom was widowed at twenty-seven. Poppy says that'll make you tough like nothing else. We moved in with Poppy above the hall after Dad died instead of going to Florida to live with Mom's mother. Mom said Grandma Carol would have loved to have us, but it was better staying here. My big sister, Camille, says that's because Grandma Carol never understood about Mom's going to college. She's heard them fight about it, too. Mom says going to college is something she needs to do to make herself better and Grandma Carol says plenty of people do real well without it, like *her*. We drive down to Florida every summer to visit and swim in the ocean, though. I'm glad Mom and Poppy never fight about school. They fight about how hard Poppy works and how hard Mom works and the right way to grow tomatoes on the roof.

Mom's father died when she was a teenager; he was a salesman—that's all I know about him. He wasn't around much. Grandma Carol showed me a picture of him once, but his face was fuzzy, like he wasn't even there. Camille was six when our dad died. She says you can get real hung up about having a dead father and that you've got to get on with life.

I walk to the open window and hear the *click, click* of pool balls in the hall below. Poppy started teaching me to play when I was four years old on the same little table my dad learned on. She said that from the start, I always had the fire. I learn from everybody, too. The guys in the hall give me pointers. I appreciate the help, but sometimes having so many teachers gets confusing.

Snake Mensker says stand up tall.

Big Earl Reed says bend down easy.

Madman Turcell says grip your stick tight.

Hank the Crank says play it loose.

"Ta da!"

Camille jumps into the kitchen with shiny pink fabric hanging all over her. Camille is designing and sewing the costumes for her high-school play and it's the only thing she ever talks about other than boys. Camille is sixteen.

"Mother," she says, twirling around, "isn't this fabric *divine?*"

Mom touches the cloth. "Very nice."

"I'm going to make matching skirts for the girls and put sequins on them for the big dance number. It's going to be heaven." Camille touches the freckles on her nose, which are just like Mom's. *"What,"* she says to me, "is the matter with you?"

"I don't like pink much."

Camille closes her eyes. "A typically limited male response. Honestly, Mickey, sometimes I wonder what you will grow up to become."

I point a potato at her. "I'm going to be nine-ball champion of the world!" This doesn't mean much to Camille. She hates pool. "And I don't like pink because there's no pink on a pool table."

"You are so *totally* alien!"

I lift my arms and give a blood-sucking vampire scream.

"Enough!" Mom shoves chicken, potatoes, and carrots into the oven.

Poppy comes into the kitchen carrying a copy of *Billiard News* and asks Camille why she's all wrapped up like a mummy. Camille says she's connecting with the fabric if that's all right, and Poppy says she'd better disconnect if she wants any dinner. Camille runs out of the room saying in case anyone hasn't noticed, she's under *massive pressure* trying to get the costumes ready for the play. Poppy takes a pan of apple crisp from the freezer and says don't worry, we've *noticed.*

Camille doesn't talk at dinner. She doesn't talk much the next day at breakfast either. Mom says it's a real compliment to Camille that the school gave her this opportunity to show the world her talent. Camille sniffs and says she's scared she'll mess up on the costumes and Mom says that's a real natural feeling. I say even if she does mess up bad, it won't be the end of the world—there's always another game.

Camille stands up. "This *isn't* a stupid pool game, Mickey! This is my *life!*" She runs out of the kitchen.

"What did I say?"

Mom shakes her head and kicks my bookbag toward me. "Go to school, darling."

I go.

Arlen gets worked up at school because Petie Pencastle tells him that Rory Magellan is planning the greatest science fair experiment in the history of Grover Cleveland Elementary. Petie doesn't know if Rory is building a chemical purification plant or an electric car.

"How do you know this?" Arlen screams.

"Because T.R. told me."

"How does he know?"

"Because Warren Eversley told him."

"Warren Eversley," yells Arlen, "is in third grade! This is not a reliable source!"

Petie shrugs. "He lives next to Rory."

"I need facts!" Arlen shouts. "Aerial photographs!"

Mrs. Riggles gets worked up talking about the Revolutionary War and forgets to give us science and reading. The best teachers don't stay on schedule. Mrs. Riggles says that some people who fight each other can become friends like America and England did. Petie Pencastle and I smile at each other. Petie tried to beat me up when he first moved to town, but we found out we had things in common, like playing pool and spitting, and started liking each other after that. I think a lot of the world's problems could be solved by a couple of guys shooting a few racks down at the local hall. Mrs. Riggles says war happens when people lose all common ground with each other.

On the way home from school I ask Arlen if he thinks Buck Pender and I are at war.

"It's a definite possibility."

Arlen starts running like a soldier with a grenade in his hand. I check the piece of cloudy sky above A-1 Locksmith for low-flying planes; we sneak behind Leon's Shoe Clinic, smelling the polish. We rip across the vacant lot beside Vinnie's Variety, staying low.

No enemy sighted.

Arlen heads home down Slocum Street. It's up to me to make it through. I turn right on Flax Street and whistle to Mrs. Cassetti, who whistles back like always. I wave at Mr. Kopchnik, who lifts an old vacuum cleaner from a woman's Chevy and carries it to his fix-it shop.

"It went *phhhit,*" the woman says, following him toward the little brick store. "Then it died."

"*Phhhit?*" Mr. Kopchnik asks. "Or *phhhit phhhit?*"

"One *phhhit,*" says the woman.

Mr. Kopchnik stops at the fire escape that leads to his apartment above the shop and shakes his old head. "That's bad," he says, giving me a wave.

Mr. Gatto sticks his head out of Cut Rate Gas and Groceries and tosses me a Tootsie Roll.

I jump to catch it. "Thanks!"

I watch Crystal's Launderette for enemy surveillance. Hard to see through the purple curtains. Crystal's giving a washer a kick to get it going. Looks clear.

I cross the street by the bus stop and head inside the heavy green door to Vernon's, where Big Earl Reed, the day manager, is picking a soft blues song on his guitar. He nods that bald head of his, lifts his bushy eyebrows, and slaps the side of the old guitar he calls Baby Gal. He got her in New Orleans. Earl and I have been friends for years even though he's fifty-three and I'm ten. His father died when Earl was two, so we've got stuff in common. His great-great-grandfather was a slave in Mississippi.

Big Earl's eyes are closed. He's told me how blues is something that grows inside you and has to spill out. If I couldn't be nine-ball champion of the world, I think I'd be a bluesman. Blues helps people understand sadness. Big Earl sang a song at my father's funeral about good men dying young.

"Play it now," I say, and lean against the counter to listen.

"Mom?"

Mom's sitting at her desk doing her college homework, which means she's got her earplugs in for total concentration. Mom started going to night school part-time to become a teacher after Dad died. He made her promise she'd follow her dream. She's going to graduate this June.

"Mom?" I touch her shoulder. She jumps sky-high.

"Try, sweetie, not to come at me from behind." She puts her hand over her heart, takes her earplugs out. "So how did life treat you today?"

There's a rumble on the street.

"What in the world?" Mom looks out her bedroom window. I look, too. The awesome green Peterbilt pulls past Cut Rate Gas and Groceries and parks. The man gets out, flicks some dirt off his Western boot, straightens his cowboy hat, and walks toward Vernon's.

"That's the cowboy, Mom! I've got to go downstairs."

"Homework first," she says.

"Mom!"

"Do it!"

I crash into my room and divide fractions like a maniac. It takes a whole thirty minutes. I turn to go.

"Check your work!" Mom yells.

"I checked it!"

This is only half a lie. I'm going to check it, honest. I race down the wooden stairs and stop at the pool hall door. I catch my breath and walk into Vernon's, not too fast, not too slow—with *attitude.*

Poppy's on the phone screaming that if somebody doesn't come fix the Coke machine that's been broke for three weeks, she's going to get a new one filled with Pepsi. I get a bead on the cowboy who's playing on table eleven, get my rack of balls behind the counter, and walk to table twelve, cool.

Snake Mensker slaps me five. "Mick the Stick," he says. This is an honor. Snake's the head stick—that's pool talk for best player. He's got a scar on his cheek that looks like a rattler. He says he got it in a knife fight in Detroit back when he was stupid.

The guy with the beard nods hello and makes a killer two-ball combo shot. I nod back and get a stick from the wall. I set up my three-bank terminator trick shot because it makes me feel tough when I make it. I put the four ball near the corner pocket, put the cue ball in place, aim my stick—

"You're going to miss it that way, son," the man says.

"I've been making this shot for years, mister." This isn't exactly true.

"You're going to come out short," he says, chalking his stick, "just to the left of the four."

I shoot, hitting the first two banks. Then the ball rolls short, just to the left of the four.

Poppy shouts, "Joseph Alvarez, don't you go corrupting my grandson now, do you hear?" She laughs when she says it.

I step back. "You know my grandmother?"

"I sure do."

You were here yesterday, I'm thinking. She didn't know you yesterday.

"Haven't been here for a lot of years," he says, and touches his beard. "Didn't have this when I last saw her and your mom. I was pretty skinny back then, too." The man stands straight up and folds his arms. He looks like a boxer. "I was a friend of your dad's, Mickey."

I put my stick down.

"We were real good friends, your dad and me. I met you, too." Joseph Alvarez puts his cue ball in place at the end of the table. "Course you were too little to remember." He lets loose a machine-gun break. I watch as three balls zoom into pockets.

I step toward him. "Did you know who I was yesterday?"

He smiles and makes the four ball in the side. "I had a pretty good idea."

"What did you mean about me winning that game?"

Mom comes downstairs at this point, lugging a bag of laundry for the launderette, brushing back her bangs like she always does. It's Wednesday, her day to do the laundry. Camille and I take turns on Saturdays. Joseph Alvarez looks at Mom and bites his lower lip.

"We'll talk about it, son. I promise. But not now."

He takes a big breath and heads right toward her. He says something to Mom I can't hear, points to his beard, and Mom about drops the laundry.

"It's me," he says. "Honest."

Mom's mouth is half-open. She's just staring at Joseph Alvarez, who brushes himself off and scratches his head. "Do I look that bad?" he asks, laughing.

Mom's trying to pull herself together, trying to smile, but I can tell she's struggling.

"We thought . . . ," Mom begins, and doesn't finish.

Joseph Alvarez's face caves in. He takes a step toward her and lets out a long sigh. "I'm sorry I let you down, Ruthie. I know I'm nine years late."

CHAPTER

I'm in the kitchen making my Mickey's Famous Double Chocolate Chip Brownies, which Mom asked me to make so that Joseph Alvarez would see the best the Vernon family has to offer at dinner. Poppy says some of the best chefs in the world are men, which proves that males can learn anything. I created the recipe myself using three boxes of brownie mix and two bags of chocolate chips. Mix this together and bake in a roasting pan. It will feed six ten-year-olds.

Mom and Joseph Alvarez are in the dining room setting the table. I can see them from the kitchen door; I'm trying to eavesdrop and bake at the same time. Mom's voice is really tense. She's telling Joseph Alvarez how she's an assistant nursery-school teacher, but when she gets her teacher's degree, she's going to teach older children who won't smear food on her clothes. She doesn't mention how she used to sometimes treat Camille and me like three-year-olds when she came home from work. Last December Camille met her at the front door for a whole week straight and said, "Mother, I just want to remind you that I am sixteen and Mickey is ten. We can go to the bathroom by ourselves and we know how to cut our meat." Mom got the idea. The only time she asks us if we have to go to the "potty" now is before a long car trip. Camille is real good to have around for some things.

Camille is wearing the silver apron she made that says A STAR IS BORN. She's making her special salad dressing with extra-virgin olive oil and red-wine vinegar.

"Do you remember him?" I ask her as Joseph Alvarez's big laugh booms from the dining room.

Camille has little memory pockets she can pull from sometimes. She shakes her head.

"What did he mean about being nine years late?"

Camille dices up some garlic. I don't know how she does anything with those long red fingernails. "I'm clueless, Mick."

If Poppy ever yells at me for being late again, I'm going to tell her she should be grateful the latest I've ever been for anything was four hours and fifty-three minutes instead of nine whole years. The buzzer goes off; Poppy's Mile High Lasagna is done. Poppy made it instead of what she usually does on Wednesday nights—teaching pool at the senior center. Poppy says seniors in America need a whole lot more pool and a lot less bingo.

We all sit down at the round oak table, which has been set special with candles and the napkins you're not supposed to get dirty.

"I do remember this table," Joseph Alvarez says, feeling one of the scratches.

Poppy smiles. She can tell you the history of each scratch on our table. Dad made the water spots when he was a boy; his brother, Ed, who lives in Montana now, put the nick in the side when he was showing off his new Swiss Army knife. Uncle Albert, Poppy's brother, made the slice in the middle when he was carving the Thanksgiving turkey and Aunt Edna kept telling him he was doing it wrong. Poppy says a table isn't worth much until it's got a few good scratches in it. She feels the same way about faces and wrinkles.

Mom's homemade herb bread is right by my place and I suck in the smell of it as Poppy says the blessing.

"Lord, we thank you for this fine food and for bringing this rascal Joseph back in our lives. We pray he won't be such a stranger." Poppy raps the table, which means she's done. Joseph Alvarez says, "Amen," and starts putting away the lasagna and talking about his trucking life and how he's just moved to New Jersey from Alaska to start a trucking business with his brother, Enrique. He says that no matter where you stand on Alaskan soil, you see mountains, big sky, and wilderness.

"It's the last frontier," he explains.

"Well, you were always looking for that." Mom says it like it's not a good thing.

He says he and Enrique saved enough money

working in Alaska to buy two trucks and they're leasing two more. He puts a card on the table:

A TO Z TRUCKING—LONG AND SHORT HAULS
—ANYPLACE, ANYTIME
1540 South Street
Cruckston, NJ 02573

| Joseph Alvarez | 201-555-0067 |
| Owner/Operator | fax 201-555-1903 |

He says his own truck's logged three hundred thousand miles and is still rolling strong. Then he says to me and Camille if we ever want to ride in it, just say the word.

Now, I'd like nothing better than to ride in that truck, except wiping Buck's face across a pool table on national television. I clear my throat.

"What did you mean about me winning that game with Buck Pender?"

Joseph Alvarez leans back near the blue-painted china cabinet, which belonged to Poppy's grandmother. "He was trying to psych you out and you were letting him do it."

"I was trying to win!"

"You bought everything that boy said, son. That's why you were sweating."

"He's a bully! You saw him!"

Joseph Alvarez shrugs. "You've got to know that all bullies want a payoff. You can't give them one."

"How?" I say soft.

Joseph Alvarez looks around the table and gets a smile from everyone except Mom. He points that long finger at me again. "You don't listen to lies. You learn to be the best at what you can do. You commit to it, you practice your rump off. You figure out the part of the game that you're best at, and you figure out why you're losing."

I feel like jumping out of my chair. "Where'd you learn to play pool so well?"

Joseph Alvarez puts down his fork. "Well now, I was lucky, son. Your dad taught me."

I slam my hand right down on my lasagna. "For *real?*"

Joseph Alvarez laughs and hands me his napkin. "He was one rough rider, too. Old Charlie wouldn't let me hang on to any of my bad habits."

Poppy slaps her side, laughing too. "That is surely right, Joseph!"

I wipe lasagna muck off my hand. I look at Mom, who's not laughing or eating. I don't think it's the talk about Dad because he comes up plenty of times and she can handle it.

"Do you play like him?" I ask.

"I play like him some," Joseph Alvarez says. "I got my game. Charlie had his."

This is too cool. I hold on to the table as everyone except Mom has seconds. I reach under it and touch the initials my dad carved there when he was my age: CMV. My heart's thumping hard.

I lean forward. "Can you help me *win?*"

Joseph Alvarez smiles big and sticks out his hand. "Son, nothing would give me greater pleasure than to—"

"I'm sure Joseph is a very busy man, Mickey."

Mom gets up and starts clearing away plates with short, choppy motions.

"No, Ruthie, really, I'd love to help."

"It's not a good idea." Mom storms into the kitchen and throws a pan in the sink.

"But Mom!"

"No!"

I feel like I just got thrown in jail.

Joseph Alvarez is looking down.

Camille is playing with her silver earring.

Poppy nudges me, nudges me again.

"Ouch!"

She points toward the pan of brownies on the server by the window like dessert is going to solve the problem. I bring them to the table and start cutting them in huge squares as this heavy feeling fills the room.

"I have never," Joseph Alvarez says quiet, "seen a brownie that big."

I hand him one. "It's the biggest brownie in America."

I clear some plates from the table and bring them in to Mom. She's fuming around the sink, shoving the little yellow rug in place to cover the cracked floor tiles. I can hear Poppy telling Joseph Alvarez how good it is to see him again and how they'd all wondered if he'd fallen off the end of the earth.

"I guess Alaska's pretty close to the end," he says loud, looking in at Mom.

"I guess it is," Mom says under her breath, and starts scrubbing a pan hard with Brillo even though it doesn't seem to need it. Her lower lip starts going, she looks hard at the yellow-and-white-striped wallpaper that she and Camille put up last summer, then runs out of the kitchen, saying she isn't feeling well, and takes that wet Brillo pad right with her.

I come back into the dining room.

"What was that about?" Camille whispers to Poppy.

"Pundonor," Joseph Alvarez says sadly, getting up slowly to bring his plate to the kitchen.

"Pundo-what?" I ask.

"Pundonor," he says. "It's a Spanish word. It means something you've got to do—a point of honor."

I can hear the Peterbilt roaring away down Flax Street. Mom never did come back out.

"Honor," I say to Poppy. "That means doing the right thing, doesn't it?"

"That's what it means."

"Did Joseph Alvarez do something wrong?"

Poppy rubs her fingers to get the blood circulating. It helps the arthritis in her hands. "Just because somebody's an adult doesn't mean they always know what to do."

"I know that."

"Your mother never cared much for Joseph's ways, and it's up to her to decide what's best for you."

"What didn't she like about him?"

Poppy thinks about that. "What bothered Ruth most, I think, was how Joseph just needed his space.

He'd go off for days, weeks, to kind of recharge, not tell anybody, and then he'd come on back to visit."

"Where'd he go?"

"I never asked him. I just respected his right to do it."

"He always came back?"

"He did. We used to kid him about where he'd go, and he'd laugh and say nothing. Your dad always called him Cowboy because he had that kind of spirit to him. He and Charlie were always working on cars, doing something automotive. Makes sense he's driving a truck, starting his business, wearing that hat. On the road's a good place for Joseph."

"What did he mean about honor?"

Poppy runs her hand through her short gray hair. "I'm not getting in this fight, young man. There's too many shadows. You just believe your mom is going to do the best thing for you she knows how to do."

"What if she doesn't do the best thing?"

"You'll live, regardless."

"If Dad was here, he'd be teaching me."

"That's right," Poppy snaps. "But you just remember, whatever happens, that down deep inside you there's a whale of a champion, just like your father."

Mom stands at the counter in the kitchen finishing her oatmeal. Camille's already left for school. Poppy's taking her morning energy walk. Mom's talking fast about how Larry Troller called this morning to tell her that last night the citizens' patrol got some drug pusher arrested who'd been using the abandoned Chrysler dealership on Krenshaw Street as his warehouse.

I'm glad about the pusher. Petie Pencastle's brother started taking drugs last year and had to go to a special hospital to not want them anymore. I made a poster in school for Health Week with a skull and crossbones on it that said BAD DRUGS ARE BAD NEWS. Mrs. Riggles hung it in the best place in the hall, right next to the water fountain.

"We're going to trumpet this all over town," Mom says. "*This* will bring volunteers in." She rinses her bowl in the sink, grabs her tan coat. "Got to run. You have a good day, honey." She touches my shoulder and heads out the back door and down the steps like Joseph Alvarez never came to dinner last night.

I shove my oatmeal away.

I can't believe she did that!

I race into my room, which is right off the kitchen, jump over my blue beanbag chair by my bunk bed, push the clothes aside in my closet, and open the secret door that leads to the roof. My room's the smallest in the house; I picked it because of the passageway. I head up the dark stairs fast, touching the wall on either side to steady myself, moving toward the strip of light under the roof door. I get to it, push the door open, and step out on the flat, black surface.

I take a big breath and let it out slow. Poppy says that helps with anger. It doesn't much today. I stare out at the stone bell tower at the Lutheran church, at the cop cars going in and out of the Botts Street police station, at the low-hanging clouds over Zeke's Towing. When we studied weather in school, Mrs. Riggles gave me an A+ in cloud recognition. The clouds over Zeke's are cumulonimbus—flat bottoms with flowing, puffy tops, the kind that bring showers.

It's warmer today. The wind picks up over Mackey's Auto Supplies and fills my windsock full. I made it with one of Mom's old nylons—attached the nylon to a wire loop, stuck that with string onto a bamboo stick, and let it fly. A garbage truck blows black smoke in the air on its way to the dump as the bells at Grace Lutheran Church start ringing.

It's eight o'clock; time to go to school.

I head down the stairs, through my closet, and down the back kitchen steps.

At school I tell Arlen about everything. He says adults need extra time to get reasonable when they've acted immature. He points at Mr. Borderbomb, the school principal, who's walking down the hall fast.

"He's wearing his mallard duck tie," Arlen whispers to me. "He's been mad five out of the last six times he's worn it."

Arlen sees patterns in everything.

Mr. Borderbomb stops at the big picture of Grover Cleveland hanging by the lunchroom. Grover Cleveland was born in New Jersey and became the twenty-second and twenty-fourth president of the United States, taking a break in between when he got beaten by Benjamin Harrison. We studied him last fall during Giants of New Jersey Week along with Thomas Edison, the inventor, Vince Lombardi, the football coach, and Joyce Kilmer, the poet. They all have rest stops named after them on the New Jersey Turnpike. Mr. Borderbomb looks like he's got gas; so does Grover Cleveland. Mr. Borderbomb yells at three kids who are making noise outside the library and tells Mr. LaPont, the janitor, that the boys' bathroom is a mess *again*.

We hide under the stairwell as he storms by. Arlen can also tell when Coach Crow is going to lose it

—usually it's right after Petie Pencastle misses his third free throw in basketball. Arlen can't see patterns in parents yet.

He also can't see why we have to sing these dumb songs in music appreciation when there are plenty of good songs around like "Ninety-nine Bottles of Beer on the Wall." Ms. Weisenberg is planning the big spring concert and the fifth grade has to sing a song about the first robin of spring. T. R. Dobbs, who has the best speaking voice, is supposed to shout, "Look, everyone, here comes a robin!" right in the middle of the song. T.R. says he's going to eat soap and puke the night of the concert so he doesn't have to do it. Arlen and I are having a slow-walking contest to music appreciation class to postpone the pain.

We get there eventually (I win) and sneak into our seats. Ms. Weisenberg stretches that long neck of hers and yells at the boys to "Sing out!" This always makes the girls laugh, especially Cindy Gunner. Then the boys have to sing our part alone, which is worse than eating creamed spinach, because Ms. Weisenberg's hands are waving in the air trying to get us to sing "fuller." We sing a little louder, which is the last thing anyone wants to do with a loser song. By the time the bell rings, the only thing we appreciate about music class is that it's over.

It's raining when school gets out. Arlen and I take the school bus home and sing "Ninety-nine Bottles of Beer on the Wall" loud with the rest of the fifth-grade boys so the girls know we can do it.

Arlen and I get off at the sixty-eighth bottle right before his carsickness hits and walk the last two blocks down Mariah Boulevard.

All day long I've been thinking how to say it.

Maybe "You don't like Joseph Alvarez, do you, Mom?"

Or "Mom, is there something about Joseph Alvarez that bothers you?"

Arlen heads off to his cousin Francine's house, where he stays after school when his parents have to work late.

"Just remember," he says, "your mother isn't going to want to talk about it. When my mom hung the beechwood kitchen cabinets too high in the Krebbs' new addition and had to rip them out and hang them lower, she wouldn't talk about it for two months."

"I don't want to talk about it."

Mom's face has that hard look it gets when she's had it; even her freckles look mad. I don't want to talk about it much either, but . . .

"You don't like Joseph Alvarez, do you, Mom?"

She stiffens. "Mickey, I've had one lousy day. We took nineteen three-year-olds to Toy Town to see how a business is run. Donny Palmer threw up on the bus. Cybil Docks and Jenny Romano had a fight in aisle twelve over the last Baby Oh-So-Sweet doll. Joshua Cohn lost his *shoes!*"

She collapses on the blue corduroy chair in the living room and covers herself with the little plaid blanket. I push the footstool over, put her feet on it.

"You don't trust him, do you, Mom?"

Her eyes crash shut. "We haven't seen Joseph for a very long time, Mickey. It bothers me that he thinks he can just stroll in here like—"

"Poppy seems to like him," I say.

Mom nods. "Poppy always did."

"Dad liked him?"

"Yes."

"I kind of like him, Mom."

Nothing.

"Is it okay if I like him?"

"It's okay," she says, rubbing her eyes. But I don't think she means it. I hear the echo of pool balls clicking up from the hall.

I say the next part fast. "Is it okay if he helps me with my pool game so I can beat Buck into the dirt?"

Mom sighs deep and looks at me. "Mickey, I understand how much you want this."

"He's the awesomest player, Mom, because Dad taught him!"

She throws off the blanket. "There are things, honey, that you don't understand. I need to think about what's right for you!"

"Winning is right for me!"

"This is not about winning!" Mom bolts up. *There are things, young man, that you don't understand!*

Mom goes to lie down in her bedroom. Since it's Friday afternoon, she says I can go to Francine's house as long as I'm home by dinner. Francine's house is a good place to go to when there are things you don't understand. Camille offers to drive me; she'll do anything to get behind the wheel.

Camille twirls up her long curly hair, sticks it under her floppy black hat, and steers Mom's old red Chevy down Flax Street. "Ugh. There are parts of this town that are positively decaying. Look at that sign over Cassetti's Bakery, Mickey. The wood's so cracked you can hardly read it."

"Mrs. Cassetti's helping her granddaughter go to college," I remind her. "She said signs cost money and everybody already knows where the bakery is."

"If Poppy just painted Vernon's purple like I've suggested, it could start a major trend."

"Yeah, nobody'd come in the hall anymore."

"A *creative* trend, Mickey. We're too limited here. Boring brick stores, apartments on top."

"What's wrong with brick?"

She sighs and turns the corner a little fast. The tires screech.

I hold on to my seat belt. "What about those new stores going up on Botts Street?" I ask her. "What about Pinkerton Park getting all cleaned up?"

"Honestly, I don't know why Mother stays here."

I look out the window at Officer Hack, who's waving from her patrol car as we drive by. I wave back.

"You do too know why."

Camille bites her lip and holds the steering wheel so tight all the rings on her fingers stand up. Mom loves Cruckston. When Dad died, people poured out to help, even folks she didn't know. We had to borrow space in people's freezers to hold all the casseroles neighbors sent. That's why Mom started up the citizens' patrol. She says at the heart of Cruckston is something that won't die—hope.

I shout to Camille to slow down, the light just turned red. She hits the brakes and almost rams a bus.

"This is close enough!" I yell. I jump out of the car and run the last block to Francine's.

"See," says Francine, holding out her official Magicians' Society card. "There's a rabbit on it. I've got to have a rabbit for my act."

Arlen and I look at the picture of a little rabbit coming out of a black hat and nod. Francine is eleven years old and the only official magician either of us knows. I asked her once if she could make Buck Pender disappear and she said she couldn't.

Francine opens her mouth and picks at her braces. "You can't play Vegas without a rabbit. I talked to Sister Immaculata about it and she said that what could really convince my parents to get me one is if I come up with a list for why I need it." Sister Immaculata is the new nun at St. Xavier's Academy and Francine talks to her all the time.

"She has a past, you know," Francine continues. "She used to work in *advertising*. It's better when nuns have a past because it means they understand life. I'm going to be a nun after I've played Vegas."

Francine adds glitter to her sign that she made out of posterboard. She's used four bottles of red glitter on it already. It says

You can read it from half a block away if your eyes are decent. Francine wants a paying magic job more than anything.

She steps back, brushes glitter off the plaid jumper the nuns make her wear, and squints at the poster. "Well," she says, "Buck Pender's been at it again." Arlen and I move closer. Buck got transferred to Francine's school in January after getting kicked out of Thomas Edison Junior High for being a scum. Francine says Catholics let anybody in. The nuns like a challenge.

Francine watches Buck's every move, too, even though he's in seventh grade and she's in sixth. "Buck took longer in confession today than anyone," she reports. "Only God and the priest know what he's been up to. *But* his parents came to school yesterday and I overheard them talking to Father Gilly about *military* school."

Francine overhears things by standing near open doors and listening.

"One that's far away," I add. "Maybe he could get transferred before the tournament."

She puts her hands on her hips. "You're going to have to think of another way to win, Mickey."

"I've thought of one." I tell about Joseph Alvarez and my mom.

Francine wrinkles her long nose. "This Joseph Alvarez smells *fishy*. I'm sure your mother is protecting you from the truth about him. He's probably a criminal. Sister Immaculata once sat next to a man

48

on the train all the way to St. Louis and they talked for two entire days and then he tried to rob her when they got off the train and she had her nun suit on! But *then* this other man came out of nowhere and frightened the robber away. Sister Immaculata got to keep her money and her life because she walks with God."

"I don't think he's a criminal," I say.

"You never know about people," Francine says. "Maybe only your mother knew his terrifying secret and she was keeping it from the family because your dad was so sick. Maybe his whole family is crazy!"

"My dad taught him how to play!" I shout. "I need to learn from him!"

Francine smiles, reaches her empty hand out to my ear, and makes a quarter appear. It's one of her better tricks.

"Just lay it on thick," Francine says, pocketing the money. "It's the only way to handle mothers."

It's so thick around here, I'm choking.

I make Mom breakfast in bed on Saturday with little sausages and my Mickey's Famous Banana Bread. All she says is that I'm a terrific chef and a wonderful son. Then she goes out for her Saturday-morning bike ride with her best friend, Serena Gillette, who taught Camille how to sew since Mom falls apart with a needle and thread. Serena and her husband are fixing up the broken-down movie theater on Botts Street. They're going to call it Gillette's Movie Palace. It's going to be the best thing this town has ever seen next to Vernon's. Serena and Mom are riding to the old clock tower near the General Tire plant and when I say that's really far for women their age, Serena slaps me on my butt with her helmet.

It's my day to do laundry. I've got to wash all Camille's neon blouses in cold water or she'll hang me out to dry. I drag the big laundry basket down Flax Street making groaning noises.

Mr. Kopchnik walks outside his fix-it shop with Cindy Winsocki, who's sniffling; he's holding her doll Matilda. Matilda's head and arms are off again. Mr. Kopchnik fixes toys and dolls for free.

"I'm going to glue Matilda up and stick her in the little bed in the back while she dries overnight. It's going to be like nothing was ever wrong with this doll."

Cindy nods and runs to her mother, who's standing in front of Cassetti's Bakery.

Mr. Kopchnik looks at me through his round wire glasses. "So, champion!" he says. "You famous yet?"

I smile. "Not yet."

"Just a matter of time," he says, and bends over halfway to watch Mrs. Petrillo stomp across Flax Street, holding a toaster.

"It's sick," she says, handing it to him. "I tried everything."

Mr. Kopchnik puts Matilda in his big jacket pocket and holds the toaster like it's a baby.

"It burns the toast," Mrs. Petrillo goes. "It doesn't burn the toast."

"You want the toast burned, Sophie?"

"I want it regular, Oscar."

Mr. Kopchnik scratches his partly bald head and smiles at the little sign in his window:

IF I CAN'T FIX IT,
YOU'VE GOT A PROBLEM

He holds the shop door open for Mrs. Petrillo.

"I never lost a toaster yet," he says, following her inside.

By the time I get the laundry done all the pool tables at Vernon's are filled with paying customers. Paying customers always get to play before me—Poppy's rule. I wait around until four o'clock, grab table sixteen by the window, and only play okay.

On Sunday Mom doesn't once ask me what's wrong even though I walk around with that miserable expression on my face that always makes her feel sorry for me. I practice pool for two hours in the afternoon, but I'm still not shooting great. My English shots are sloppy. English is the spin you put on the ball to get it to line up for the next shot. Buck's watching me, laughing every time I miss.

I think he'd look real nice in a military-school uniform.

I can hear him laughing all the way through Monday.

In school Mrs. Riggles tells us about the Minutemen, who were volunteer soldiers who fought against the British in the American Revolution. They trained fast, were ready to fight "at a minute's notice," and pushed back the British in the first battles of the war, Lexington and Concord. I'd like to be a Minuteman.

My mom probably wouldn't let me do that, either.

Rory Magellan is acting like he knows the secret of the century, and it's making Arlen crazy. Rory's one of those smart kids who makes sure everybody knows it. He's got a pinched-in face and looks like he just took a big breath. Rory's sitting on the front school steps during recess talking loud with his fourth-grade friends about the anemometer he made, which measures how fast the wind is blowing. This year Rory's mother is organizing the science fair.

"You know what this means, don't you?" Arlen screams.

Petie Pencastle and I look at each other.

"It *means* that he'll get the best table for his experiment. It *means* he'll know everything before I do! It *means* she'll pick the judges!"

"So what?" says Petie. "You won the last two years and your mother didn't organize it."

Petie doesn't understand how bad Arlen wants to win. No one's ever won the science fair ribbon three years in a row. Arlen storms off saying his mother never volunteers for the right things at school.

"She's the Health Week mother," he says, groaning. "She brings *raisins*."

After school, Arlen and I head back to his house to work on our science fair project, "The Amazing Secrets of the Pool Table." Arlen wanted to call it "Death-Defying Secrets of the Pool Table to Stun and Amaze Your Friends," but Mrs. Riggles said it was better to use one big adjective and wow them with our findings. We are developing this in utmost secrecy in Arlen's bedroom with Mangler standing guard. Arlen heard from Petie Pencastle that Rory Magellan has spies *everywhere*. Arlen says once your scientific secrets leak out, you can forget about your enduring place in history.

53

I think learning the laws of the universe is a whole lot easier than trying to understand mothers.

We're laying out the poster that says

> THE LAWS OF THE UNIVERSE ARE EVERYWHERE
> YOU LOOK, EVEN IN PLACES
> YOU WOULDN'T EXPECT.

Arlen is drawing an okay universe with shooting stars that look like pool balls. I'm doing the lettering on Isaac Newton's Laws of Motion, which he figured out three hundred years ago to explain the way things move. We put them partly in our own words.

I'm drawing the first law in red:

> EVERY OBJECT STAYS IN A STATE OF REST OR
> UNIFORM MOTION IN A STRAIGHT LINE UNLESS
> SOME OUTSIDE FORCE CHANGES IT.

In pool talk this means a pool ball isn't going anywhere unless it's hit by something, and once it starts moving, it needs something to stop it like a rail, another ball, or the friction of the cloth table.

I do the second law in blue:

> THE ACCELERATION OF AN OBJECT IS IN
> PROPORTION TO THE STRENGTH OF THE FORCE
> ACTING ON IT AND THE DIRECTION
> OF THAT FORCE.

That's a fancy way to say that how hard you hit a ball will be how fast it's going to move, and the less it weighs, the faster it will go.

I do the third law in green:

FOR EVERY ACTION THERE IS ALWAYS AN EQUAL AND OPPOSITE REACTION.

A cue ball stops dead when it hits another ball straight on.

There's a knock on the door. Mangler starts squealing. "Friend or foe?" Arlen shouts.

"Cousin." Francine walks in wearing lime-green tights and a long T-shirt with sparkly stars. When the nuns aren't watching she lets loose. She stares at our poster. "It needs glitter," she says, flopping down. Her face gets serious. "What was the worst moment of your life that you can remember? Everyone has to answer."

Arlen says when Mangler got hit by that motorcycle and was lying on the street bleeding and had to have surgery.

I say when Poppy and I got robbed two years ago by that man with the ski mask and the gun who said if we called the police, he'd come back and get us.

Francine says it was when she realized she'd never be as successful in life as her big sister, April.

We're all just sitting there with our worst moments.

"April's president of her junior class, she's on the debate team, she's *beautiful*." Francine covers her big ears with her thin brown hair. Buck Pender called her Dumbo once and she ran all the way home crying. "I just want to be the youngest magician to ever play Vegas and outdo April in anything. Is this too much to ask?"

This is why Arlen and I like Francine. She cares as much about her magic as we care about math and pool. We've been hanging out with her for years, too, even though she's a girl. She's got other friends her age, but they live across town.

I say April can't do magic tricks.

"She could if she wanted to."

Francine takes out a deck of cards and does her magic shuffle. "Pick a card, any card."

I pick one. She touches her forehead. "The Amazing Francine will now tell you what card is in your hand." She stops to think. "The three of hearts."

"No."

"Ten of diamonds?"

I shake my head.

"Ace of spades?"

"King of spades. You were close."

Francine throws her cards on the floor. Card tricks are the weak point in her act. "I need a rabbit!" she wails. "Animals help you connect with an audience!"

Mangler starts squealing. Mrs. Pepper shouts that we have to take him outside before the noise shatters the crystal.

Arlen grabs his new book, *Harnessing the Memory Power Within You,* and we head outside. "This wouldn't happen in a tree house," he says sadly.

Francine looks at Arlen's memory book and groans. We've tried all kinds of systems to help him remember. Color-coded ones, numbered ones in base ten and base three; we made a chart to keep track of everything he owned, but Arlen lost it.

Arlen thumps the book. "Do you know that memory is based on association? I just have to find symbols for the things I don't want to lose."

"*Bookbag . . .*" Arlen turns the word over in his mind. "When I think of *bookbag* what do I see?"

"Death," Francine offers. "If you lose your book-bag again, your father will kill you."

"School," I say.

Arlen shakes his head.

"Homework?" I try.

Arlen leans against the oak tree, thinking hard. "Prison," he says. "No—I'd never remember that. Punishment. Misery." He closes his eyes. "Wood!"

Francine and I look at him, confused.

Arlen's jumping around, hugging his memory book. "That's it! The paper in books is made of wood. Tree houses are made of wood. Every time I see wood I'll remember!"

I'm standing behind the counter with Poppy. She just had a wart removed and isn't too chirpy.

"Spit it out," she says. "You're dragging around like a flea-bitten dog."

I say how's a kid supposed to feel when he can't get the straight scoop on the one thing in the universe that could guarantee his future as pool champion of the world?

She shoves a rack of balls at me. "You're sure not going to improve that game of yours bellyaching here."

I kick at a dustball and head for table eight, passing Buck in the process. He's wiping the cloth with Marcus Denny. He taps the nine ball in for a win and says he has to go.

"I got my first lesson with *Carter Krantz*. . . ."

I stop dead in my tracks. Carter Krantz! He's the sixth-ranked man in the world for nine ball. He's the best player in the state. Marcus is saying Buck sure is lucky—his dad wouldn't even buy him his own stick, much less private lessons with Carter Krantz.

Private lessons!

I rack the balls, trying to pretend I don't care. But Buck knows. He swaggers over, puts his hand on the table, and feels the cloth.

"Don't even bother practicing, little boy," he sneers at me. "It won't do you any good now."

I'm in my room, flopped in my beanbag chair, feeling the blackness surround me. I look at all the pieces of paper stuck with little colored pins on my bulletin board. It's my autograph collection of all the pool greats I've ever met: Steve Mizerak, Johnny Archer, Allen Hopkins, Buddy Hall, Earl the Pearl Strickland, Nick Varner, Dallas West. I've seen them play exhibition matches. They're so awesome. I hug one of the big, round nine-ball pillows Camille made for my birthday. I read what I've written:

Dear Mr. Alvarez,
Buck Pender has hired a world-class pool coach and you're the only person who can help me now. I need a coach pretty bad or everything I've been working for is over. Please talk to my mother. Please do whatever you have to do so that I can learn how to win. I'm pretty sure my dad would have wanted me to learn from you.

Sincerely yours,
Mickey Vernon, age ten

I'm not sure about the part about my dad, but when I called Francine and read it to her over the phone, she said it could be the deciding factor. I put it in an envelope, write URGENT AND PERSONAL EMERGENCY on the front, and copy the address from the A to Z Trucking card Joseph Alvarez left at dinner.

"It'll get him," Francine said, "even if he is a criminal."

It's been two days since I mailed the letter.

Buck is definitely getting better.

I ask Mom if she's figured out what's right for me yet. This is a mistake. Her face gets purple. Her green eyes go into little slits. She says when she's figured it out, she'll let me *know*.

I'll be in college, probably.

Arlen, Francine, and I are at table seventeen. Arlen's wearing his favorite T-shirt; it reads R U GIFTED? He's rubbing my shoulders like a boxing coach.

"You're going to make it happen, champ, right? You're going to focus, ram those balls into pockets. You can do it because you're the king! Let's hear that thunder break. . . ."

I lean over the table to shoot and look over at table fifteen, where Buck Pender is knocking in balls with ease, stretching his long arms across the table. I think he got taller since his lesson.

I put my stick down.

"What?" Arlen asks.

I wipe my nose. "I'm worried, okay?"

"Not okay," Arlen says. "You think a mathematician starts thinking he can't finish a problem? You've got to think positive, Mickey."

Big Earl Reed puts up the tournament poster in the window.

> WE'RE LOOKING FOR THE BEST AND THAT COULD
> BE *YOU!*

I walk up to the poster and touch the *you*. Buck heads out the door, looking like he eats cement for breakfast.

Big Earl touches my shoulder. "World's full of Bucks, Mickey V."

"One's too many."

"First one just helps get you ready for the others."

"Yeah . . ."

Mrs. Riggles said the same thing at school—every battle the colonists fought in the American Revolution helped them get ready for the next one. That's why the best soldiers are the "seasoned" ones. Then she told us about a homework assignment that's due next month. We each have to pretend we're a soldier in the Revolutionary army and write a letter home about our experiences in battle. We can pick any battle, Mrs. Riggles said, and passed a box around. We all took slips of paper that had our pretend soldier's name and rank. Mine said "Lieuten-

61

ant John Q. Milner." Arlen was mad; he only got a private first class.

"Write your soldier's name down," Mrs. Riggles said. "Just think about him for now."

Arlen leans against the pool table and reaches into his bookbag, which he hasn't lost for days. "A perfect one-inch-square cube," he says proudly, holding up a little cardboard box. "I finally got it right. With this, I can win."

He takes out a bag of jelly beans, places a few in the cube. He shakes it, adds two more beans. Arlen is set on winning the jelly bean guessing contest at the mall and the hundred-dollar gift certificate. The sign in the mall said it's the biggest jelly bean display in America.

"You're cheating," Francine says, picking up cards. "The sign said to *guess* how many jelly beans are in the fish tank, Arlen, not figure it out to the square inch."

"Mathematicians don't guess," he says, adding a final bean to the box.

"Well, if you ask me, it's not fair. *I* guessed and I won't tell you how much. Maybe I'll win."

Arlen empties the cube and counts the jelly beans. "Thirteen," he says. I write it down. "They're the exact same size as the ones at the mall."

Francine touches her silver cross necklace. "Sister Immaculata says that God knows everything. That means God knows how many jelly beans are in the tank."

Arlen says we have to go to the mall and measure the jelly bean guessing tank. This is one of those times that God isn't telling.

62

Francine stands up fast. "I'm going home. A future nun can't be involved in anything dishonest." She pops the rubber band on her braces, grabs her mountain bike, which Poppy lets her keep inside the front door for safety, and heads out.

Arlen holds up his one-inch cube like it's a diamond. "We're going to be rich."

Poppy drives us to the mall in her beat-up beige Rambler, which she says she bought "when dinosaurs roamed the earth." The black vinyl seats are held together by duct tape, which nobody minds except Camille. Poppy doesn't like new things much. To her, everything needs to be broken in, including pool tables. Poppy says she'll meet us outside Pearlman's World of Fashion and goes to Sears to buy herself a man's lumberjack shirt since the one she's had for twelve years finally wore out.

Arlen and I head for the jelly bean guessing tank, looking down as we walk past Ladies' Underwear. It took four store managers two hours to count all the beans—that's what *The Cruckston Comet* reported. Arlen takes out his tape measure and starts moving fast.

"Length—twenty inches."

I write this down.

"Width—twelve inches." Arlen puts his tape measure over the side of the jelly bean guessing tank, making sure no one is looking. "Depth—ten inches. Glass thickness—eighth of an inch. Bottom thickness—quarter of an inch." Arlen snaps his tape measure shut.

We walk out of Pearlman's World of Fashion and sit on a bench in the mall. Arlen gets out his mechanical pencil and pocket calculator and starts figuring.

"Subtract a quarter inch from length, depth, and width for glass and bottom thickness," he says. "Multiply length, depth, and width together for volume. Multiply volume by . . ."

"Thirteen jelly beans," I remind him.

"For . . . 29,414 jelly beans!"

He checks his numbers. I check his numbers.

"You've got it," I say. "Without using the glass thickness, we would have been off by 1,786 beans."

The paper that shows how he did it is awesome.

Arlen's face starts glowing. We head back to the jelly bean guessing display.

"Would you boys like to take a guess?" asks a thin saleswoman.

Arlen looks at the jelly bean guessing bowl like he's never seen it before.

"Go on," the woman says. "Take a big guess now."

Arlen touches his sunglasses. "29,414, ma'am."

The woman takes a sidelong glance at Arlen and writes that down. "And would you like to guess, dear?" she asks me.

"Same," I say.

"Pardon?"

"29,414."

"That's what he said."

"We're partners," says Arlen.

How to Win the...
Jelly Bean Tank Contest

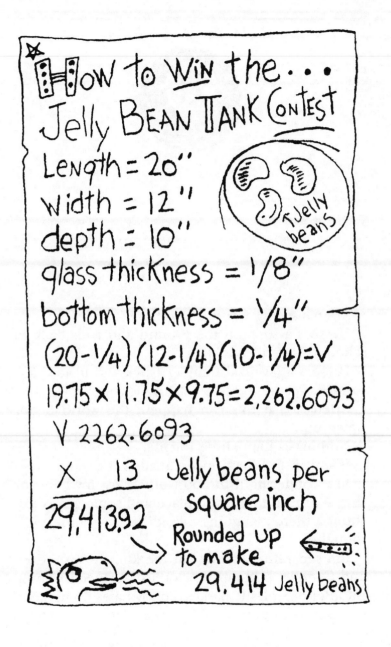

Length = 20"
Width = 12"
depth = 10"
glass thickness = 1/8"
bottom thickness = 1/4"

$(20-1/4)(12-1/4)(10-1/4) = V$
$19.75 \times 11.75 \times 9.75 = 2,262.6093$

V 2262.6093

$\times$ 13   Jelly beans per
——————   square inch
29,413.92
   → Rounded up
     to make
        29,414 Jelly beans

Arlen's seeing wood everywhere.

He sees a stick on the ground and runs back to school to get his bookbag.

He sees a Jaworski Lumber truck and heads back to wherever we were to get his jacket.

Arlen says if this can happen, the world better watch out.

Nothing is happening for me.

It's been five days since I mailed the letter.

I'm wondering if the post office lost my letter or they sent it to the wrong place and some guy is just sitting there laughing, reading my innermost thoughts.

I'm separating laundry in the kitchen with Mom and Camille, putting the clothes that need ironing into Poppy's plastic basket. Poppy hates doing laundry and loves to iron. She's an ace at it, too. Poppy says anyone can do laundry; ironing takes a strong heart and skill.

"Mother, you have *got* to be kidding!"

Mom just told Camille that she has to start paying for the gas she uses in the car, which means that Camille has to keep baby-sitting Rodney Huffington, who is five years old and tries to handcuff her to the refrigerator.

"Motherrr," Camille says, "Rodney is going to injure me someday, I swear!"

"We have insurance," Mom says. "Everything costs money, Camille. I save every month for your and Mickey's college education. This is how you can help." Mom holds up my favorite jeans, which got two more holes in the knees when Petie Pencastle shoved me off the gravel hill at recess.

"Mom!" I blurt out. "I've got to talk to you—it's *so*—"

The phone rings. Camille runs to answer it in case it's one of her potential boyfriends.

"Hello . . . ," she says with that little thing in her voice.

Camille looks weird. "Mom—it's for you."

I shove as much popcorn in my mouth as it can hold from the bowl on the table.

Camille winks at me and stretches the phone toward her. "Joseph Alvarez."

My body freezes.

Mom's moving slowly to the phone. I'm making noises through the popcorn. She closes her eyes, takes a deep breath.

"Yes . . . ," she says flat into the phone.

"We'll surround her," Camille whispers to me. We move in close.

"Joseph, I appreciate that, but this isn't a good time for me. . . ."

I'm trying to chew what's in my mouth, trying to suck on it, anything to get it down my throat. I'm praying he'll keep on talking, say something really smart that will—

"All right," Mom says into the phone, "go ahead."

Please, God.

Mom leans against the stove, listening. I'm trying to read her face. Camille pretends she has something to do by the stove. Mom gives her a dirty look and turns away.

"I know . . . ," Mom says to the phone.

Know what?

She's listening again for a long time. I finally swallow.

"Please!" I shout.

She throws up her hands.

I grab some paper and write

MICKEY VERNON, POOL CHAMPION OF THE
WORLD—IT'S ALL IN YOUR HANDS NOW

I hold it up to her.

She sighs deep. "You have to understand," she says into the phone, "that it was so hard here . . ."

I drop to my knees right in front of the stove and look like I'm praying. Camille's moving in behind her. Mom covers the receiver.

68

"Do you two *mind*?"

I'm lying on the kitchen floor now whispering, "Please, please!"

Mom's listening some more. Then she says, "Yes, Joseph, I've heard you." She sighs. "All right . . . goodbye . . ."

She turns to me. "That was quite a performance."

I get up and brush myself off.

"Sit down," she says, looking gray.

Camille and I sit.

"I meant *Mickey*." Mom gives Camille a little push out of the kitchen and leans against the stove, folding her arms. "I know how much you want Joseph to help you, Mickey, and I'm sure I'd feel the same way if I were you. But there's something you need to know."

"Okay."

Mom brushes her bangs back like they're heavy. "You need to know that when your father was dying, he asked Joseph to look in on us from time to time, just to make sure we were okay. I'm sure your dad saw things in Joseph other people . . . *couldn't*. He asked Joseph to get to know you and help you. I never felt comfortable about this because Joseph always had trouble staying around, but he promised left and right that he'd be there for us. He wasn't." Mom steps toward me slow. "He moved out to Los Angeles after your dad died, which was certainly his right." Mom is looking at me all sad and worried. I hate it when she looks like this. She touches her head the way she does when she gets a headache.

"Mickey, we're always honest with each other, right?"

"Yeah."

"I want you to know how much it bothers me that Joseph didn't fulfill his promise. He was your dad's *best friend*. He didn't call us. He didn't bother to write once in nine years. He just moved away. And now he's back. Nobody's perfect and we need to try and forgive people when they're not. But I've got to tell you, Mickey, I don't know if Joseph is the kind of person you can count on." She takes a big breath. "I've known someone else like this. He never changed."

"Who?"

Mom sighs and looks down.

I'm sitting at the table looking at the mud spot on my sneaker.

"Are you going to ask him why he didn't call us?"

"No."

I don't know how hard it was when Dad died. Camille said the hospital bills kept coming and the insurance wasn't enough. I'm thinking about Dad and how he trusted Joseph Alvarez to do the right thing. He doesn't seem like a guy you can't trust, but like Francine says, you never know about people.

"I don't want you to get hurt," Mom is saying. "I don't want you to go blindly into working with someone whose history has been that he rarely stays and finishes the job. Are you ready to accept that?"

"He might have changed," I say.

70

"He might have," she agrees, "and he might not have."

I swallow big. I don't know what to do. Dad wanted him to help me. Dad taught him how to play. Isn't that important too?

Mom shivers and pulls her robe tighter, but it can't cover the worry in her face.

"Could I just try, Mom? If he hasn't changed, I'll blow it off. I swear."

Mom closes her eyes for a long time. The leaky faucet's going again. Poppy keeps trying to fix it. "He said he'd be back in town on Saturday, Mickey. He has to go to Texas."

"It's okay then?"

"For now."

Mom leans back. Her face looks beat. "But if I don't like what I see just once, and I mean once, I'm pulling the plug. If Joseph can't make it work it's not because of you, Mickey, it's because of him."

I'm waiting for Saturday to come.

If Joseph Alvarez shows up I'm going to take that real positive. If he doesn't, it could mean lots of things because everyone knows truck drivers get stuck in bad traffic.

Arlen said his uncle Chester went to live in Milwaukee and didn't contact anyone in the family for seven years and then showed up with a wife, two kids, and ten pounds of bratwurst and everyone forgave him.

Francine said to wear a bulletproof vest and to call 911 if Joseph Alvarez does anything fishy.

I promised I'd call.

Rory Magellan did something stupid—took apart his cousin Marna's new stereo to see how it worked and couldn't put it back together. Arlen said a *true* scientist always draws diagrams when he's disassembling something so he can put it back. Marna told

Francine about it and Francine's almost got her convinced to find out what Rory's planning for the science fair. Arlen says if Francine can pull this off, she'll be one of the great nuns of all time. Arlen forgot his bookbag twice this week; he's going nuts waiting.

Mrs. Riggles announced that so many kids are participating in the science fair, it's being moved from the gym to Town Hall and Mayor Blonski is going to present the awards. Arlen throws back his head.

"My parents didn't vote for Blonski!" he tells me, groaning. "We had a KROLL FOR MAYOR BEFORE IT'S TOO LATE poster right on our front lawn."

Arlen and I are walking Mangler across the covered footbridge over the connector to the New Jersey Turnpike, which is a block from his house. The noise is so loud. I'm looking down at all the trucks roaring by. None are as cool as the big green Peterbilt.

"How do you know when you can trust people?" I ask Arlen.

He looks down at the freeway sign, TRENTON—KEEP RIGHT, and shivers. Arlen went to Trenton for the semifinals of the state geography bee last month and lost on Addis Ababa, the capital of Ethiopia.

"I guess it's by what they do," he says, glaring at the sign.

We've been studying about George Washington, who always did what he said he was going to do. They asked him to be king of America and he said no. "A man of unshakable honor," Mrs. Riggles called him.

We cross the footbridge onto Clyborne Street, which is as far from home as my mom lets me go without an adult. The April buds are just forming on the trees. People on Clyborne are serious about their trees because the leaves help soak up the noise from the interstate. Mangler's walking proud, getting the usual attention.

A woman puts down her shopping bag. "Is that a pig?"

"I believe it is, ma'am," says Arlen.

"Well, isn't that *something*," says the woman, leaning down to look at Mangler, who snorts. "It doesn't look dirty. I thought pigs were dirty."

Other people start gathering round. Arlen goes into his pig speech about how pigs are really misunderstood and have been forced by humans to live in slop.

"They're highly intelligent," he says to the group. "Abraham Lincoln had a pet pig."

"I didn't know that!" says a man.

No one knows this except Arlen. He takes a raisin out of his pocket, holds it just out of Mangler's reach.

"Dance," he says to Mangler.

Mangler gets up on his hind legs reaching for the raisin and takes a few small steps toward the food. At home Mangler does this to music. Beethoven's Fifth is his favorite. Arlen gives Mangler the raisin and the crowd starts applauding.

"Good pig," Arlen goes, patting Mangler's head. "That's a real good pig."

Petie Pencastle, Matt Fitz, and Jeremy Dozier turn the corner by Jude's Grocery. They empty out their pockets, shaking them down to the lintballs, and put their dimes and quarters on the sidewalk. Arlen and I smell money and head over.

Petie's counting by the sidewalk grate. "We got a dollar ninety-three," Petie says, scratching Mangler's head. "You guys got any?"

Arlen and I come up with eighty-eight cents. Petie's squinting in the sun trying to add in his head.

"Two dollars and eighty-one cents," Arlen says.

Petie kicks at the grate and does some figuring. "Candy bars are forty-five cents each. That's enough for us to get six. Okay?" Petie, Matt, and Jeremy head for Jude's front door with the money.

Arlen tells Mangler to sit. "I can buy us more candy with less money," he says. "You guys like M&M's?"

"Sure," Petie says, "but they're forty-five cents a bag too."

Arlen hands Mangler and his leash to Matt, the youngest, and heads inside Jude's, past the BEST BETS OF THE WEEK sign, to aisle six. CANDY. He picks up a one-pound bag of M&M's.

"Six bags of M&M's at one point sixty-nine ounces each is ten point fourteen ounces total and costs two dollars and seventy cents. For two dollars and seventy-nine cents, we are now going to buy *sixteen* ounces of M&M's."

Petie and Jeremy are silenced by genius. Arlen buys the candy and we follow him outside. Arlen sits on the LOANS WHILE U WAIT bench by the bus stop; he divides the candy into five piles and keeps an extra handful as a "management fee."

Arlen and I head toward Pinkerton Park and the

75

new baseball diamond. "With math," Arlen says, scarfing chocolate, "you can have a real good life."

It's Saturday, 12:23. I've been on table five since nine this morning. I haven't gone to the bathroom or anything because I want to be standing here looking tough when Joseph Alvarez shows up. Arlen went to Francine's to throw himself on her mercy. Camille dragged the laundry basket through Vernon's to wish me good luck, which was real nice. I look out the window for the hundredth time. Mrs. Cassetti's sweeping the welcome mat in front of her bakery again, which means business is slow.

Man, I hope he's coming.

I hope I've got what it takes.

I hear the truck before I see it.

I quick chalk my stick.

Tap the balls down perfect.

Flick a piece of lint off the table.

My heart's thumping crazy.

I'm waiting.

Where is he?

Maybe it wasn't him. Maybe I saw one of those mirages people get in the desert when they want something bad.

But I didn't. Joseph Alvarez bursts through the front door. He's wearing his big Western hat; his boots look spit-shined. He's carrying a leather pool cue case and he looks like somebody you don't mess with for one minute. He tips his hat to Poppy, who smiles as wide as I've ever seen her.

I run up to him, grinning.

"You ready?" he asks.

"He's a bomb waiting to go off," Poppy says, cracking open a roll of quarters.

I bring him to table five.

He puts his hat on a chair, opens his case, and takes out an awesome pool stick—a Balabushka. I've seen pictures of those in *Billiard News*.

Man . . .

He screws it together. It's got different shades of wood around the handle in a triangle pattern. He rolls the cue ball across the table to me.

"Well now, Mickey Vernon. Let's see what you can do."

"Okay!"

I plant my feet strong, push up from my heels, focus on smashing the cue ball with my power break.

Pow.

It's more like a dud. The cue ball rolls four inches.

I bite my lip and look down.

"Happens to everybody," Joseph Alvarez says. "Try again."

I try again and don't get much.

"You nervous?" he asks.

"No." I wipe my sweaty hands on my best jeans.

"Slow, disciplined, focused," Joseph Alvarez says, moving the two ball near the side pocket. "Just tap her in."

I push into the shot too hard and scratch—the cue ball plops in the corner. A scratch in pool is a bad thing.

Joseph Alvarez gets the cue ball, hands it to me.

"Shoot anything," he says. "No big deal. Have fun with it."

I try a couple of bank shots, but I miss those too. This is probably the worst I've ever played. I slap my stick on the table.

"Don't go doing that, son. It's not the stick's fault. Pick it up."

I swallow hard and pick the stick up.

"I'm sorry," I say. "I don't know what's wrong."

Joseph Alvarez looks at me, scratching his beard. "I need to talk to your mom."

He's giving up on me already! "She's at the library all day studying. I'll do better—I promise!"

"It's not about that."

He walks to the counter and says something to Poppy, who looks at me for a long time and nods.

Joseph Alvarez walks back, slaps on his cowboy hat. "Let's go," he says, heading for the door. "Poppy said it was okay."

"Where are we going?"

"To your first lesson."

We're moving down Flax Street in the Peterbilt, sitting high.

The steering wheel is made of wood. Two little cowboy boots hang down from the rearview mirror. The seats are covered in dark leather.

Everything is better in a truck.

We roll by St. Xavier's—the dark old stone makes it look like a castle. We head past the police station with those big steel doors that look like you're walking into a refrigerator. The Peterbilt moves on, churning up a cloud of dust near the cars locked behind the chain-link fence at Zeke's Towing.

I can see the flat roof of Grover Cleveland Elementary. "That's where I go to school," I say.

Joseph Alvarez slows down and gives it a good look.

"The clock in the front's always ten minutes slow no matter what the principal does to fix it."

"You like school?"

"It's okay. I don't like oral reports or grammar."

"Not hot for those myself."

He turns down Botts Street and smiles at the new stores going up. Gillette's Movie Palace is getting a coat of bright yellow paint, which should do Camille a load of good.

"This was all junk when I was around last," Joseph Alvarez says. "Old machine shops, a dumpy liquor store, rats in the alley. Folks work hard here to make things better."

People look as we roll by. A lady lifts her baby up to wave at us. We wave back; it's like being in a parade. I'd sure like to see Buck right now.

I say I think I'm riding in the best truck in America.

"I'm glad you think so, son. Some drivers beat a truck to death and wonder why it's not performing for them—you've got to treat it nice and it'll take care of you. I try and let my truck tell people who I am."

Joseph Alvarez pulls into the parking lot of GameLand, which is where Arlen had his tenth birthday party. It's got miniature golf, shooting, archery, and all kinds of games inside, except pool. We have to park near the street, there's so many cars.

"Out," he says.

"What are we doing here?"

"Only way I know how to teach pool is how your dad taught me."

Joseph Alvarez takes off his hat and starts up the

80

walk, which is painted with big red footprints. I run to catch up. We stop at the little white booth.

"Full game package or a la carte?" asks the woman chewing gum behind the cash register.

"The works," Joseph Alvarez says, taking out his wallet.

I take his arm. "They don't have any pool tables here. . . ."

"That's right."

We walk through the main door, which makes a laughing sound when anyone comes through it. Kids are screaming, bells are going off. We stand there looking at the red, white, and blue rooms jutting out like boxes in a maze. A little boy starts wailing when his father says he's out of tokens. A tired mother is counting the little girls around her.

"She's going to lose it," Joseph Alvarez says to me. "On three. One . . ."

The woman throws down her purse.

"Two . . ."

The woman throws back her head.

"Bingo."

She starts shouting that no one is moving *anywhere* at this birthday party until she finds *Ashley*!

We laugh good and walk through the arcade of blinking video games into a smaller room with Ping-Pong tables. Joseph Alvarez picks up two paddles.

"Your serve," he says, tossing the little white ball to me.

I miss the catch. "I'm not good at Ping-Pong."

"Serve."

I serve bad. Joseph Alvarez returns the ball, bouncing it right on the line; it sails past me.

"Zero–one on the serve," he says as I run to get the ball. "Serve again."

I do and it's worse. He nails it past me like I'm blind.

"Why," I ask, "are we doing this?"

"Focus on the ball, son. Zero–two."

We play to zero–eleven. It doesn't take long. Joseph Alvarez writes our names on a scorecard and under his he puts a 1 for winner, which sure seems like rubbing it in.

"Know why you lost?" he asks.

"Because I'm ten."

"Nope."

"Because you're better."

"Because I make those spin shots you haven't figured out how to hit yet."

Like I said.

Joseph Alvarez beats me seven to zip and each time he wins he puts a little mark under his name. I say shouldn't we be getting back to the pool hall for practicing and he looks at me hard and says, "You can't learn to win, Mickey, until you learn how to lose."

The words hang over the fat red nose of the painted clown poster.

We walk through the arcade to the snack bar. The man behind the counter has a T-shirt with a hot dog on it. Joseph Alvarez buys two Mountain Dews and says, "How are you at archery?"

"Awful."

He nods, steers me to the archery section, and hands me a bow and arrow. "Shoot," he says.

Well, I'm standing there like a ding-dong trying

to put the arrow in and hold it up; the arrow keeps falling out of the bow and every kid there for a birthday party is laughing at me. Joseph Alvarez stands next to me, stretches his bow back, and hits a perfect bull's-eye. He says to hold the bow steady, and I say I think I got a bad bow. I'm sweating now because people are waiting in line for their turn and I'm sure everyone thinks I'm stupid. I try to shoot and the arrow makes a little leap toward the ground.

"Focus," he says to me. "Concentrate on the arrow, the bull's-eye, making it happen."

I can't!

"C'mon. You can do it."

I throw my bow down and storm off past the shuffleboard court, the miniature-car raceway. My head's pounding and my brain's melting. Joseph Alvarez comes alongside me and hands me a golf club.

"Miniature golf," he says. "I'll spot you ten strokes."

"I want to go home."

"Why?"

I glared at him. "I'm sick of losing, okay?"

"You lost today, Mickey, but what did you learn?"

"Nothing."

"Really? You didn't figure out how to beat me?"

I haven't figured out anything except that I've probably never lost so much in my whole life as I have in this stupid day. He steers me to the golf course. I'm pretty good at miniature golf; most pool players are.

Joseph Alvarez steps up to the first hole with the little hill and almost makes a hole in one.

"C'mon, Mickey. Shoot."

I can't beat him, even with the ten-stroke spot. My ball keeps getting stuck in Aladdin's mouth on the fifth hole and I overshoot the eighth hole because the windmill messes me up. We play three rounds of eighteen holes and each time my score gets a little higher until all of a sudden on the ninth hole I realize how the greens roll—all of a sudden, I can't miss. I beat him bad on the last round with a hole in one on the seventeenth, right across the little bridge that's guarded by the ugly troll, and totally miss the water. Joseph Alvarez's ball hits the troll's stomach three times in three games and plops in the water. But I see the roll and I'm ready. I tell him to forget the ten-stroke spot, I can win on my own. I nail my ball right through the grizzly bear's mouth on the eighteenth.

"Good game," he says, shaking my hand. We walk up to the snack bar and get double cheeseburgers with chocolate shakes. I'm eating mine, feeling tough.

Joseph Alvarez looks at me and smiles. "Charlie Vernon's rule number one in playing pool and anything else—if you can figure out why you're losing, you can figure out how to win."

We leave GameLand after two more Ping-Pong matches that I still lose, but my backhand shots are definitely getting better. I figure out that Joseph Alvarez likes to play the corners and he's expecting me to do it too, so every so often I blip one just over the net and he has to reach like mad to return it. His face gets all stern and I know I have him. I also figure out that if I just keep watching the Ping-Pong ball, not anything else, I can usually hit it. Joseph Alvarez says I'm a natural-born all-around athlete, which no one has ever said to me since becoming the world champion of nine ball has been taking up most of my time.

I say Ping-Pong isn't so bad.

"Great way to clear your mind and work on focusing," he says. "Winning, losing, focusing, sportsmanship, patience, determination—it's all there, son, played out on that table."

We're heading toward Vernon's in the Peterbilt, moving past the abandoned Chrysler dealership on Krenshaw Street. The afternoon shadows make it look haunted. I'm looking in the windows where the new cars used to shine through, trying to picture where that drug pusher has his business.

Joseph Alvarez stops at a red light. "You know what I found in Alaska?"

"No . . ."

"In Alaska I found *ganas!*"

"Huh?"

"It's a Spanish word for desire—the thing that makes you want something so bad you go after it with everything you've got."

"Ganas," I say.

"That's it. Nothing important works without it."

"You've got to find the *ganas* to get better, to push yourself. See, I always loved trucks—everything about them. I'd climb into one and feel this energy pumping through me. But I didn't have the money to get a truck, to start my business. I had to make it happen. So my brother and I got good-paying jobs in Alaska. We worked overtime for two years, saving, living cheap. I had the desire. It was in my blood." He pats the dashboard. "I bought this rig. I don't imagine any cowboy loved his horse more."

"Are you a cowboy?" I ask.

Joseph Alvarez tilts back his hat and smiles. "My great-great-grandfather was a *vaquero*—that's cowboy in Spanish. He rode horses from Mexico up through Texas and into California. A *vaquero* sat on a horse for three days straight not talking to anybody except his animal, which isn't sprightly conversation. He and I, we've got the same spirit for the open road. Lots of truckers do."

"That's why you wear the cowboy stuff?"

"That's why I wear it. To remind myself of the spirit inside. Now that's what we've got to find in you—and that will make way for the natural pattern for your game."

He pulls out a pack of Wrigley's Spearmint and gives me a stick. "It'll come," he says. "I'm sorry about those nine years, son. I feel real bad I didn't come by sooner."

I'm looking out the window, watching a bus pick up an old man with a cane. "How come you didn't?"

"Your dad dying just laid me out. I drove away from it—as far as I could go."

Joseph Alvarez steers the Peterbilt onto Mariah

Boulevard, heading for Vernon's. "Your mom's got a right to not be happy to see me."

I look at him. His arms get stiff holding the wheel. His face looks so sad.

I want to tell him it'll all work out.

But I don't know that it will.

It's Sunday. At church I prayed that Mom would get happy about seeing Joseph Alvarez and that Buck would go to military school. After lunch I went to the hall to play nine ball with Marcus Denny, who's thirteen years old and makes big-time stupid mistakes. I'm beating him, too. Joseph Alvarez said he wanted to just watch me play. Part of me wishes he wasn't watching.

This isn't my best game.

I've missed two bank shots and I almost blew an easy tip in the corner. My hands are sweaty and I keep glancing over at Buck, who's looking like a tank. The red shirt's hanging in the window right by the Knights of Columbus dinner dance poster; the dance was last week. Poppy's slow in taking things down.

I want it so bad.

I take a big breath, wipe my hands on my jeans,

and bank the eight ball at a forty-five-degree angle; it just makes it into the side pocket. I look up at Joseph Alvarez, who's sitting on the bench against the wall, stroking his beard, not frowning, not smiling. I shoot the nine ball at the side pocket and miss, but Marcus misses too. I tap it in the corner.

Yes! That's a win.

"Good game," I say to Marcus, and shake his hand, looking up at Joseph Alvarez, who stands up and leans against the table with his hands in his pockets. Marcus walks off.

Joseph Alvarez says, "You could have played that cleaner."

"I won. . . ."

"You did," he agrees, "but you almost didn't."

I kick at the floor because I just won and I'm used to grown-ups falling all over themselves about how good I play. He throws the balls back on the table.

"Shoot something," he says.

I bend over to hit the three ball.

"Shoulders and neck can't move when you stroke," he says. "It messes up your aim. Try again."

I freeze my neck and shoulders, bend over—

"No." Joseph Alvarez gives me a light push against my shoulders and I crash forward. "Tighter," he says. I squeeze my shoulder blades until they hurt. "Tighter."

"I can't breathe!"

"You've got to break those bad habits before they become a part of you. Shoot."

I shoot and miss the three.

"Follow through," he says. "Don't hurry it, just let it come natural."

I'm standing here suffocating, pinching my shoulder blades together, and he says be natural. I try it again, follow through, and nick the three.

"Better. Do it again."

I do it again and again and again.

"Feel the difference?" he asks.

I'm rubbing my neck and shoulders. I feel the difference—*pain.*

Joseph Alvarez turns to me and puts a quarter on the rail of the table. "On bank shots," he says, "you're getting the angles pretty well. You've got to focus on hitting the ball clean. Shoot the quarter."

"What?"

"Aim at it. Shoot it medium hard. Like this." He rams the cue ball into the rail and the quarter jumps off.

I try. The quarter doesn't move.

"You'll get it."

I try harder and don't get it.

"Focus on exactly where you want the cue ball to hit," he says. "Your dad had the best focus of any pool player I've ever seen."

"Really?"

Joseph Alvarez sticks quarters up and down the rail and starts shooting the cue ball at them, making them jump. "Charlie could block out anything and anybody that was trying to throw his game."

"How'd he do it?"

"I asked him once. He said he just closed the

blinds in his mind and played." He makes the last quarter jump and hands it to me.

"Time for homework." It's Mom. Her voice is flat. She's standing at the table looking like she'd rather be anywhere, including the North Pole.

Joseph Alvarez shoves his hands in his pockets. "How are you, Ruthie?"

She holds the mega-flashlight they use on citizens' patrol. "Tired."

Joseph Alvarez looks lost.

"You want to play some nine ball, Ruthie? I mean, you used to have a serious break. I remember that time when we were all—"

Mom shakes her head and motions me toward the stairs. I put my stick on the wall.

"Here." Joseph Alvarez hands me one of the quarters. "You ace that homework. Okay?"

My fist closes around it. "Okay."

I'm thinking we should invite him up for something to eat.

But being ten, I'm powerless.

I tell him thanks for everything, really, and follow my mother up the stairs.

I'm standing in the kitchen holding a banana. Mom just announced that she has homework, *important* homework—she's writing a paper called "Educating the Reluctant Thinker." It's about how kids don't always want to learn and what teachers can do about it.

Give them a day off, if you ask me.

Then she storms out of the room yelling at me to do *my* homework and she isn't going to tell me again. I do my genuine karate kick that T. R. Dobbs taught me and eat the banana.

Dad's favorite fruit was bananas. Poppy said when I was small I used to leave a banana out for him at night, in case he wasn't getting enough food in heaven.

I sit at the kitchen counter and open my vocabulary book to lesson thirty-four. The first word is *confound:* "To cause to become confused or bewildered."

I've got to use it in a sentence. I write:

"The mother's strange actions confound the world champion pool player."

You hardly ever see something in vocabulary that applies to real life.

School isn't going so well.

We have a substitute teacher because Mrs. Riggles has to go to the doctor to get her pregnant stomach checked—not the good kind of substitute that knows how to teach, either, the bad kind that thinks we're babies. She makes the whole fifth grade sit on the floor in a circle for "Self-esteem." We have to imagine we have a box in our laps with something inside that will make us happy. Arlen asks how big the box can be and can his have holes because without them his tarantula is going to suffocate. Everyone starts laughing and Petie Pencastle asks if his box can have meat in it to feed the twelve-foot man-eating crocodile. The substitute's face gets red and she makes us sit quietly for ten minutes while she stares at us. I imagine the red championship shirt is in my box, but I don't tell anyone.

Lesson three with Joseph Alvarez isn't going so well either. He starts by telling me to brush my hair even though I brushed it this morning already to go to school. Then he says to tuck in my shirt and wash my hands.

"You're a pool player, Mickey. That's something to be proud of."

We're at table nine. It's hard to feel proud when you're playing like dirt.

"Slow, disciplined, focused," he says. "Nope, you've got too much swing on your stroke."

He stands behind me and shows me how to hold a cue stick like I've never held one before in my life.

"You hold it like it's a butterfly you've got in your hand that you don't want to escape," he says. "You're gripping too tight."

"That's how I've always held it."

"I know. But it's going to mess you up later on. Look." He shows me how he does it.

I'm gripping the thing, feeling my muscles twingeing.

"Relax, it'll come," he says.

I tense.

We move into the second hour of our practice and Joseph Alvarez is racking the balls, telling me that learning a new way of playing is going to be hard. "In the beginning, Mickey, you're going to play worse."

Worse!

"I haven't got time to be worse!" I look over at Buck Pender, who's smirking and nailing long shots, and here I am back in kindergarten.

Joseph Alvarez is saying how I've got to not focus on winning.

"You said if I can figure out why I'm losing, I can figure out how to win."

"Yes I did, and I want you to tuck winning behind your brain for now. We'll bring it out when it's time. You concentrate on getting better. Be satisfied with that."

Is he kidding?

"You can't find the fun in playing if you're always hung up about winning," he says. "See, Mickey, you've got to learn to relax. People who are coming down hard on themselves about each shot, each thing they did wrong, each missed ball, are tense. Tense people make mistakes."

I'm working hard to untense and it's giving me a headache.

I'm doing everything wrong.

I can't grip the stick right.

I can't shoot the balls right.

I feel like I've never played this stupid game.

"I'll tell you something about your dad, Mickey. He had fun when he competed. He played just as hard when he was winning as when he was losing."

I lean over the table and miss an easy corner shot. I can't believe it. The tournament's six weeks away and everybody in the hall's watching me and thinking how skunky I'm playing!

"Let's stop for now," he says.

"No, I can do it."

"Man's got to know when his horse is beat for the

day. Sit down." Joseph Alvarez points to table seven, where Buck's just started playing Big Earl's son, Perry, who is fourteen years old and won the tournament last year.

"Watch," he says.

Perry gets one in on the break and Buck tries sneering, but Perry doesn't pay attention, gets five more in and misses. Buck swaggers to the table saying how winning is going to be a cinch.

Perry says, "Then do it, man."

Buck snorts, gets the seven ball in and misses the eight.

Perry smiles—drops the eight and nine in easy for a win.

Buck says, "You got lucky."

Perry's racking the balls. "Think so?" He rams the cue ball on the break and gets one in.

Buck's face is getting pale. I could watch this all day. Perry's got a tough shot that he misses, but he doesn't leave Buck much either.

Joseph Alvarez says just loud enough for me to hear, "That's how you play Buck Pender. Nice and cool. You don't say much. You don't leave him much. The cooler you get, the hotter he gets."

Buck hits the five, six, seven balls in. Buck's gotten better, I can definitely see this, but he can't throw Perry and that's throwing him. He blows the bank on the eight. Perry knocks the eight and nine together like nothing.

"You handle Buck like that next time," says Joseph Alvarez softly.

I'm thinking this is a pretty stupid way to spend my time, waiting around until Joseph Alvarez comes back on Saturday from his trip to Texas with a truckload of canned tuna fish, which he said will make him popular with every cat in America. He told me to practice what he's taught me, especially the quarter-jumping exercise, which he says is the best he knows for focus.

I've been aiming at quarters for three days and not connecting like Joseph Alvarez said I should.

Julian Meister slaps me on the back and hands me a Coke. He and Mom went out on a date once; Mom said once was enough. I'm not sure if he's being nice to me to get to my mom. Some men do this when you've got a pretty mom, but kids always find out in the end. Mom's old boyfriend Kevin took Arlen and me to Dr. Death's Haunted House on Halloween. We were walking through it scared because something was making noises weirder than Mangler. We stepped in glop and Dr. Death came out of the shadows and grabbed us. Kevin, who'd been through twice before said, "There. That's the end." But it wasn't, and Kevin knew it. This blood-soaked guy comes out in a mask covered with chains, howling, and we tore out like bats with Kevin laughing behind us. I never trusted him after that. Mom didn't either even though he sent her roses to apologize. Mom kept the roses and told Kevin to take a hike. Mom's not dating anyone now, which is okay by me.

I put another quarter on the rail as Francine and Arlen walk into the hall. Francine's face is all sparkly, which means she's got a secret.

"Sister Immaculata was right," she whispers. "We will reap what we sow."

"What?"

"Buck Pender got the Good Citizen Award of the Week at school yesterday in assembly." She waits for me to sit down hard. "He supposedly collected more canned food for the hunger drive than anyone, but then Sister Immaculata found Theresa Raster's initials on twelve Chunky Soup cans that Buck said were his and she made him give back the award and apologize to the whole school in assembly. You had to be a lip-reader to get that apology. It just goes to show that nuns have power." Francine takes a pad and pencil from her pocket. "Watch your back, Mickey. He'll do anything to win."

I look over at Buck on table three. He doesn't look like he's ever apologized for anything. He stares back at me with cold, mean eyes. I chalk my stick, lean over table sixteen, and shiver.

It would be nice if Arlen and Francine were cheering for me, but that's not how it's going. Arlen's reading his memory book for the third time. He's seeing wood everywhere—toothpicks, Popsicle sticks. He's only forgotten one thing in two weeks—his homework—and his father says, "Well, well," now when he comes home for dinner. Last Saturday we actually heard the sound of a hammer and nails.

Francine is making the list for her parents on why she needs a rabbit. She draws a line through her first point, IF I DON'T GET A RABBIT I'LL ABSO-LUTELY DIE.

"How 'bout, if I don't get a rabbit, I'll be unfulfilled?"

Arlen nods. "Your creativity will dry up, too."

"Yes!" Francine writes furiously. "And it could stunt my growth. Hidden anger does that, you know."

I aim at the quarter, miss for the zillionth time, and stomp my foot.

"Rabbits are clean and quiet," she says, writing madly. "They don't bark, they don't bother anyone, they require less care than other kinds of animals. Their droppings can be used to fertilize gardens. I read that in a book. That one's for my mother."

"Vernon," I say to myself, "if you can focus you can do anything. . . ."

I get a bead on the quarter and shoot the cue ball one last time. It hits the rail; the quarter jumps perfect.

"I did it!" I shout.

Arlen leans forward smiling. "Do it again," he says.

I concentrate and do it again.

Yes!

Buck Pender, Good Citizen of the Week, comes over, sneering. "What are you doing, *Vernon?*"

Arlen folds his arms.

Francine folds her paper.

I take a deep breath and focus on the quarter, hoping I can ace it now. I aim my stick, ram the cue ball to the rail. The quarter jumps!

I look right at him. "I'm making money dance, *Pender.*"

Buck backs off a half-inch. "It looks stupid!"

"Looks cool to me," says Arlen.

"Totally," says Francine.

I look up and love what I see.

Buck Pender is gone.

I'm telling Mom what a great guy Joseph Alvarez is every chance I get, putting extra emphasis on how responsible he is and how I'd trust him with my whole life. Mom and Serena are at the dining room table, drinking tea and laughing. Mom's showing the new photographs she took at nursery school.

"The kids are so cute when they bring their treasures in for show-and-tell. Jimmy Johnson used to hold out a pinecone in the beginning of the year and sit down fast. Now he marches up front and says, 'This is my truck; don't touch it.'"

Serena smiles at me. I say if anybody's interested, Joseph Alvarez is teaching me better than anyone's ever been taught. Mom shifts funny in her chair.

"He's definitely changed, Mom. You don't have to worry."

She bites her lip and looks at Serena, who starts stuffing blue papers in citizens' patrol envelopes. "Let's just take it slow, Mickey."

If we take it any slower, it's not going to be moving.

I ride my twenty-one-speed super-rock-jumper mountain bike that I got for my birthday to Arlen's.

Not much is moving over there either.

Francine says there must be some strange chemical in Cruckston's water supply that's slowing parents down. She gave her parents the list on why she wants a rabbit twenty-six hours ago and hasn't heard anything.

"It's only two pages," she shouts, "not counting the title page I did in glitter!"

She flops down by the oak tree in Arlen's backyard and Mangler starts squealing. Mangler's real nervous. Mrs. Bellweather started frying bacon next door and the smell of it carries, especially if you're a pig. Mangler goes into his hole to wallow and covers his head. Arlen and I took a blood oath never to eat bacon. We didn't actually want to bleed, though, so we used ketchup.

Arlen says if Francine's parents say no to the rabbit she can use Mangler in her act.

"No one wants to see a pig come out of a hat!" she screams.

"A pig," Arlen screams back, "is better than a rabbit!"

"I have to be able to lift the animal, Arlen! Is there no one in this world who acknowledges my true calling?"

Arlen lets loose one of his famous burps, and I shoot one back at him, but Francine doesn't pay attention.

"Some people," she says, "never discover their true purpose in life. Others, like me, have somehow always known."

She snaps her fingers and a fan pops out of her sleeve. She walks off fanning herself, leaving me and Arlen to burp alone.

It's Saturday. I've got quarters hopping like frogs on a pond. Joseph Alvarez says I'm the fastest study he's ever seen.

Ganas!

He says I've got it in my blood.

He tells me the story of his great-great-grand-father, the *vaquero*, who killed a bear that had come into his camp once, panicking the horses. He looks at Buck, who's smirking. "There's always something sniffing around trying to scare us when we're moving forward, son."

Ganas.

I've got to keep practicing.

I start getting up half an hour early in the mornings and talk Poppy into letting me shoot a few racks before I leave for school. I'm pushing so hard, my blisters have blisters.

Joseph Alvarez is giving me everything he's got. I'm getting it, too: follow-through shots, spinning the balls with English, playing for position, safety shots, which put the cue ball in a difficult place for your opponent. I'm holding my stick like a butterfly, springing it into action.

Every time Joseph Alvarez comes over, Mom makes herself scarce. It bothers him bad, but he keeps coming to help, just like he promised.

Poppy said Mom's got him frozen in time, but it's not her whole fault.

"I don't get it."

"That's all that's right for me to say." Poppy flipped open her *Modern Maturity* magazine, which meant our talk was over.

I look at Joseph Alvarez now, standing there at table six, dead on his feet. He said he hit some nasty traffic going south and stopped to help a woman whose car had spun off the road.

"You've got to help people when the road's your home," he says, and tells me how he drove all night long from North Carolina to get here.

"It would have been okay if you were late."

He waves it off. "On the break," he says soft, "you've got to find more power."

He lets loose his machine-gun break, but it doesn't have the same crack it did last week. Six in the corner. He nails the one. "Try to shoot quick," he says. "You don't lose your focus that way."

I try shooting fast and get all mixed up.

"Just do what I say," he says, irritated.

I bite my lip and blow three shots.

Joseph slams his hand on the table. "You're going to have to do better than that."

I say maybe he needs to go home and get some sleep and—

"I'm doing the best I can for you, son! If you're not going to listen, there's not much I can—"

"I'm listening! I'm just not getting it!"

Joseph Alvarez is squinting his eyes like he's got a headache.

"Okay," he says, patting my shoulder. "Okay."

Mom walks into the hall, sees us, looks down, and starts up the stairs.

"Ruthie!" he calls after her, but she's gone.

Joseph Alvarez's shoulders sink into his chest. "That's enough for today," he says, packing up.

"No," I say. "I've got to practice. I've got to get better! Can't you help me some more?"

"I haven't got any more. I need space." He holds up his hands and backs out the door.

CHAPTER

I tell Camille to keep her stupid face out of my business.

I tell Poppy and Mom there's nothing wrong with me and can't a guy have some time alone without everybody bugging him?

I don't tell anyone that I cried last night or that I shout at Petie Pencastle to get his smelly body away from me at recess or that I get a D on the surprise spelling quiz because I'm not paying attention.

Mrs. Riggles asks me what's wrong since I'm usually a good speller.

I don't tell her.

On the way home from school I kill two beetles because they're ugly and crawling on the same sidewalk I'm walking on.

It's all Mom's fault for acting so mean to him!

I'm in my room with a stomachache. I shine up

the quarter Joseph Alvarez gave me and put it on my desk next to my toad skin and my Replogle globe that I got from my uncle Ed for Christmas. I am very good at geography and can name all fifty states alphabetically and every major river in the Western Hemisphere. I came in second at the Grover Cleveland geography bee next to Arlen, who always comes in first because he's gifted. I would have held on if I'd remembered that the Arabian Sea is bigger than the South China Sea. Arlen remembered. He only has a bad memory for things you can lose.

I run my finger down the globe through Illinois, Missouri, Arkansas, and into Texas.

I don't know where he is.

Worse than that, I don't know if he's coming back.

"What we need," shouts Francine in the middle of Pinkerton Park, "is a planet where kids can live when the adults in their lives aren't being fair!"

Arlen and I nod. Francine has just decided to stop speaking to her father until she graduates from high school. She plops down on the tree stump right next to the little patch of ground where I buried my turtle Boris in a little Frosted Flakes box after he died. Boris was an excellent turtle. The daisy seeds I planted over him never grew.

"It's going to be a little tough," she explains, "us living in the same house and all, but when he said I couldn't have a rabbit, no matter what my list said, well, I'm sure I don't have to tell you that something inside me died."

"You won't graduate for seven years," Arlen says. "You'll talk to him before then."

Francine shakes her head. "I have nothing more to say. I was even going to call the rabbit Lester after him—that's the ultimate compliment, you know. He said that April's cat couldn't handle living with an overgrown rodent and *he* didn't want another animal smelling up the house. He's destroyed my entire career and doesn't care." Francine's eyes are wet. "I'll go right from high school to the convent. I'll never play Vegas!"

Arlen says adults don't realize the power they have over us.

I don't say anything.

It's been three days and I haven't heard anything from Joseph Alvarez.

I want to tell them about it, but I'm afraid if I say it with words, it will make it all the more true.

I'm heading out the front door for school, feeling not much like going. I walk past Cassetti's Bakery and the caramel sticky buns in the window. The smells don't even make me hungry. Mr. Kopchnik walks down the fire escape from his apartment and unlocks the door to his fix-it shop.

"So, champion!" he calls to me.

I lift my hand in a quick hello and keep on walking.

"Hand me the adjustable monkey wrench, will you?"

107

"Huh?"

A dirty hand waves from underneath Mom's old Chevy, which is parked across from Crystal's Launderette.

"Get the wrench, Mickey."

Joseph Alvarez is lying underneath Mom's car!

I see a bunch of tools on the street. I get the wrench.

"I'm fixing your mother's car."

I'm standing out on the sidewalk as he's grunting and rolling around under it.

"That's really nice!" I say.

"I'm hoping it'll make a difference."

I'm hoping too. If he sticks some money under the hood, it might help.

"There." Joseph Alvarez rolls out from under the car, covered with grease. "Let's start her up."

He's standing there all big and dirty and I want to shout that it's really good to see him.

"I'm sorry about the other day, son. Tiredness just got the best of me."

"Where'd you go?"

"Ohio. Had a load of cable to deliver. I should have called you."

He starts the car, lifts up the hood, and listens to the engine. "No breaks in the sound," he says to me. "She's running good now." He wipes his hands on a towel.

Just then Mom heads out the door, lugging her bag of puppets for the nursery-school kids, and nearly keels over when she sees us.

Joseph Alvarez wipes his face on his sleeve. "I

didn't know how to fix things between us, Ruthie, so I thought fixing your old car here might get the ball rolling."

Mom takes a big breath and looks down.

"That's kind of you," she says.

"It *really* is," I say.

He goes and revs the engine. "New belt, oil change, sparks. I've got my good points."

"New belt?" Mom walks over to him. "You mean I don't get to wake the entire neighborhood in the morning starting it up?"

Joseph Alvarez opens his hands and grins. "They're going to have to get alarm clocks like everybody else. I had to jimmy your lock and hot-wire the engine, Ruthie. Hope you don't mind."

Mom swallows big. "It's that easy to break into my car?"

"Only if you know what you're doing."

Mom reaches to shake Joseph Alvarez's hand and gets a fistful of car grease. He starts laughing and hands her the towel. I'm just smiling away and Mom wipes some grease on my nose.

Joseph Alvarez leans against the car. "I couldn't help thinking how Charlie and me used to fix those old cars."

Mom smiles sad. "Sometimes I'd wonder if I was married to a whole man or just those feet of his hanging out from underneath cars."

"You remember the McCoy brothers?" Joseph asks.

Mom groans.

"You remember how they drove that old Chrysler

Charlie got running for them all the way from Detroit to make the funeral?"

Mom nods. "A fifty-seven Imperial. Bright yellow. It broke down going into the cemetery. Johnny Mc-Coy pushed it while his brother steered so they could stay in the funeral procession. He said the only man who could keep it running was Charlie."

Joseph Alvarez is looking up to the sky. "Johnny was going to leave it there by the grave as a tribute. He said Charlie would have liked it better than flowers."

"He would have, too," Mom says.

I've never heard that story. I've heard about the funeral, though. Poppy said all Dad's pool player friends brought their sticks to the church and when the casket was carried out, they rapped the handles of their sticks over and over on the floor in the pool player's applause. It's the greatest honor a player can get.

Mom gets up, swings her big black purse over her shoulder. Camille calls it the Black Hole. Things go in there and never come out. "Well, guys, I've got to go to work." She motions me to come. "I'll drive you to school, Mickey." She stands there a minute, gets her car keys. "Thank you, Joseph."

"Anytime."

Mom and I get in the Chevy. Joseph Alvarez bunches up the greasy towel.

Mom concentrates hard on the road and drives off.

"Boy," I say, "it was really nice of him to do that, huh?"

Mom's holding the wheel tight. She stops at the

110

red light by Jacoby's Pest Control. Jacoby's new sign has a rat on it the size of Arlen.

"Yes it was." Mom rubs her forehead. "Fixing a car is a nice thing, Mickey, but it doesn't fix everything."

Mom's hanging on the sidelines watching Joseph Alvarez and me play. I even get her to play a rack of rotation pool with us, which she hasn't done in forever. Mom can't bank shots for anything. I beat her bad. She says I'm an awesome player and getting real fine coaching.

"Thank you for what you're doing," she says to Joseph Alvarez.

"Thank you for letting me, Ruthie. I could give you a couple of tips on a better way to hold the stick. . . ."

"That's all right, Joseph. . . ."

"Wouldn't take much, Ruthie. You're holding it a little high, which is throwing your aim a bit and—"

"No thank you."

Joseph Alvarez is going to Buffalo tomorrow with a load of motor oil and then halfway across Canada, which he said might take two weeks. This isn't great news, because, as far as I know, Carter Krantz isn't going anywhere.

"You just practice with all you've got."

"I will."

"I got one more thing for you to work on, but you don't do it at the table. You practice clearing out your mind and focusing. Shut out the world, shut out the noise, shut out all the things in you that say you can't do it."

"Blinders," I say, "like my dad."

"You've got it." He gives my hand a firm shake. "Well, it looks like you've found your *ganas*."

I smile big and say I sure have.

"Then you let it drive you," he says. "And start playing other people, Mickey. Good to get a lot of game experience before the big day."

I nod.

"But don't play Buck," he advises. "It's not that you're not good enough, just don't give him the edge, you know?"

"Yeah." I want to give him a hug goodbye, but that wouldn't be cool.

"We'll practice when I get back."

"Okay," I say.

Joseph Alvarez tips his hat and heads for the door. I run after him.

"Drive careful," I say.

"I'll do that, son." He looks down smiling, gives me a good hug, and heads out the door into the night.

* * *

It's seven days since Joseph left and I'm getting good. Everyone can see it.

I think Buck's nervous.

Joseph sent me a postcard from Toronto, Canada, that said to not look at anybody else, just worry about which ball I'm going to shoot next. "Pool games are won one ball at a time," he wrote. I taped it to the base of my Replogle globe and say, "Pool games are won one ball at a time," every night before I go to bed.

The tournament's four weeks away and I think I'm pretty close to ready. It's feeling more like spring now—you can almost go outside without a jacket. Arlen's had to stay after school every day this week to get his enrichment needs assessed because he's gifted.

"They don't want me to be bored," he explained.

"How come?"

"They're afraid of what I'll do."

The days blend into each other. I'm charting Joseph's trip by the postcards he's sending.

Ottawa.

Winnipeg.

Moose Jaw.

Medicine Hat.

Mom's impressed that the postcards keep coming. I say I think that's the sign of a really responsible person, don't you, and she says maybe. Big Earl's been playing me, and Poppy's taken extra arthritis medicine and shot a few rounds of straight pool. Straight pool's a hard game. You've got to call

114

your shots—that means saying which pocket the ball's going to go in when you hit it. Poppy never got into nine ball. You play her in her hall, you play her game.

Snake Mensker touches that rattler scar on his cheek and says I'm becoming downright deadly even though he still beats me pretty bad. I wipe Petie Pencastle over the table and blow off Danny Couriter and Nick Savlanas. I'm playing for serious position now and controlling my game. I even won one game off Perry to his five, which really says something. Perry's helping me like he helps everybody else. Buck's practicing death drills, gunning for me.

"Don't pay any attention to him," says Perry.

"I'm not."

I look over at Buck, who's half laughing. "Where's the cowboy, *Vernon?*"

"Just ignore it," says Perry.

Buck walks over, rolling up the sleeves of his shirt, planting his workboots right in front of me, and leans up close to my face.

"I said, where's that stupid cowman of yours, *Vernon?*"

Perry says, "Get lost, Buck."

I look right at him. "Take back what you said!"

"I don't take nothing back!"

"He's a better coach than you'd know what to do with!"

"Oh yeah?"

"*Yeah!*"

"Prove it, *Vernon!*"

Buck storms over to table eight and stands there. "You show me how good he coached you, little boy!"

Perry's standing in front of me telling me not to listen. "Joseph said not to play him, Mickey. You got to save it for the tournament."

"Chicken?" Buck sneers at me.

"Rack 'em!" I say.

There's a story about my dad when he was twelve and a man in the hall challenged him to a game. Dad ran ninety-seven balls before missing and the man just sat there and kept asking, "What's inside you that lets you do that, young fella?"

Dad said he guessed it was that he wanted it so bad.

Ganas.

I rack the balls on table fifteen. I want this bad.

Buck wins the toss and gets to break. My heart's thumping in my stomach. People are beginning to gather around the table. Petie Pencastle, T. R. Dobbs, Shelty Zoller.

Wham! Buck crashes the cue ball down the table and slams the balls apart. The two ball zooms into the corner pocket.

"You can't beat me, *Vernon!*" He makes the one ball in the side.

I look right back at him. "Yes I can!"

But it's like everything Joseph Alvarez taught me went down the sewer.

My hands are shaking.

My palms are sweating. Buck makes another ball and misses an easy bank.

"Didn't leave you anything," he says, snarling.

"Yeah you did."

I bend over the table. My brain is fogged in, my heart is feeling crazy. I bank the four in the side in a really good shot. I nail the five, the six. I miss the seven.

"Tsk, tsk," he says. "You're history, little boy."

Buck makes the seven in the side and stands over the eight like a vulture over a dead animal. I'm losing to him again.

I beat Perry once. Buck can't beat Perry and I'm losing to him again!

He beats me one game, two. I bend over to break. I make the eight ball, miss the one.

Buck whispers, "So where's the cowman now to help you?"

"Stop it!"

I fly at him, pushing him down. I'm punching him, kicking him. *"Stop it! Stop it!"*

Guys are trying to break it up. I'm going to get him! Hurt him! We're punching each other on the floor; he throws me off. I land hard on my hand.

"Ahhh!"

Perry runs over.

I see Big Earl's worried face over me.

"My hand!"

I can't lift my left hand, can't bend it.

Big Earl's helping me up. I'm dizzy. The pain is bad. He shouts at someone to find my mother. T.R. tears upstairs. Earl says if I got to throw up, go ahead and do it.

Mom rushes into the hall.

"Dear God!"

Earl and Mom help me out to the car. We're going to the hospital.

I'm crying, "My hand! He broke my hand!" as Mom rams her old Chevy through traffic.

The doctor in the long white coat stands back and adjusts the splint on my left hand. Her face looks tired. She says she's got a boy just my age, like that's supposed to make me feel better. Two nurses help a man with a bloody eye lie down. Mom is standing next to the doctor looking plenty worried.

"That's a mean sprain you've got," the doctor says. "You're lucky it didn't fracture. Are you right-handed or left?"

"Right."

"Well," she says, "at least that's something."

"I'm a pool player!" I shout. "I've got a tournament in four weeks."

She shakes her head. "No pool for three to four weeks, Mickey."

"I've got to practice!"

"Not with that sprain," she says firmly. "You've got to let it heal."

I flop back on the hospital cot. "The tournament . . ."

The doctor sits down. "I'm sorry about that, Mickey. But that hand is a mess. I don't want you using it for *anything*! We'll check you in three weeks."

"That's not enough time!"

I close my eyes and try to push back the tears.

I might as well be dead for being so stupid.

Mom puts a hand on my shoulder and I just lose it, crying and sobbing like a baby.

Mom drives me home. I can't talk. We pull up in front of Vernon's and see the poster for the tournament in the window.

WE'RE LOOKING FOR THE BEST AND THAT COULD BE *YOU!*

I close my eyes—I can't look at it.

It won't be me.

Poppy's all upset and Big Earl is saying, "Okay now, you're going to get through it."

I don't tell him he's wrong.

I'm not going to get through it.

To beat Buck I have to practice every day!

Camille comes over and hugs me, which she hasn't done for a long time. She makes me her special hot milk chocolate with little marshmallows, but I can't eat the marshmallows because I need a spoon and I'm using my good hand to hold the mug.

I can't put my pajamas on without everything hurting. I get put to bed like a baby with the medicine the doctor gave me for pain. Nothing ever hurt worse. Mom pulls the covers over me like she did when I was small. I feel like my whole wrist has been chopped off.

Mom touches my head. "Oh, sweetie . . ."

I bite my lip and start to cry.

"I have nothing smart to say, Mickey. I just want you to know that it's not going to hurt forever. I know it seems like it will, but it's not." She kisses my forehead. "Keep that hand elevated. That's what the doctor said."

I can't believe I didn't listen to Joseph!

It's been a long, mean school week.

I sleep a little and wake up and the pain's still there, hovering over me like a thick, dark cloud.

I failed Joseph Alvarez, failed the Vernons.

And the postcards keep coming.

From Thunder Bay: "Remember to center-stroke the ball."

From Toronto: "Remember—easy stroke, easy win."

I'm not winning anything!

I can't get my coat on without help. I can't get my bookbag on my back without someone lifting it up there because I have to wear a stupid sling.

"I can do it myself!" I scream at Mom when she tries to help me.

"Sit down," she says.

I sit, but I don't want to hear.

"Let me tell you about something that I am well acquainted with, Mickey. Disappointment. When you look it in the face, admit how much it hurts, when you can forgive the people involved, including yourself, you can move on." Her face looks gray. "I don't always follow my own advice. I wish someone had told me this when I was your age. It would have made things—"

"I'm okay," I lie, trying to zip my jacket.

Mom's eyes are so sad, they take over her face. "Think about what I said."

I'm too busy being miserable.

I can't take gym.

I can't do good work on my Zulu warrior mask in art because I need my left hand to hold it steady while I'm painting.

I'm researching my soldier letter. Arlen and I both picked Valley Forge as the place where our soldiers were stationed. It was such a bad winter for the American army: not enough food, cold weather, sickness. They'd lost some important battles, too. All their hope was gone while the British hung out in Philadelphia, warm and well fed. History sure can be hard. I'm trying to picture Lieutenant John Q. Milner, wondering how he felt.

I'm pretty sure my wrist is never going to get better. Everybody keeps asking me how I hurt my hand.

I'm sick of telling.

Arlen and I are painting the poster, THE AMAZING SECRETS OF THE POOL TABLE. Arlen's really worried because Francine talked Marna into spying on Rory and the news is not good. Rory's building a five-foot erupting volcano that's getting delivered to Town Hall in a truck.

"How," Arlen shrieks, "do we compete with a volcano?"

I shake my head and look at my bandage.

I come home from school and go up the back way so I won't have to walk through the pool hall. I stick cotton balls in my ears so I can't hear the *click, click* of the pool balls below my room. Everyone's doing the chores I can't do—Poppy gets more cooking and vacuuming, Mom takes out the garbage, Camille gets more laundry. Camille's getting sick of it, too.

"I know you can't help it," she says, coming back from Crystal's with the basket of folded clothes, "but I have a *life*. I have a *fashion debut* I'm trying to get ready for."

"I'm sorry."

Then she goes into her room, where she stays up late and sews. I'm replaying every dumb move I made with Buck—it's like a movie running through my head.

Mrs. Cassetti is bringing me cookies from the bakery. Mr. Kopchnik asked if I wanted to help him take apart an old vacuum cleaner. Mr. Gatto said I could have any candy bar I wanted every day until I was better.

I just want my hand back.

It's purple and swollen and I feel the hurt going up my arm to my elbow. Sometimes kids push past me in school and bang my hand without meaning to and I have to stop where I'm at until the pain passes.

Arlen's upset. He's forgetting things again. He lost his Red Sox cap, left his bookbag in the park, forgot his vocabulary sheet three days running.

I'm not helping him remember like I should.

I'm not much good to anybody, that's what Camille says. She's been in a foul mood; she messed up on one of the costumes for the play and had to fix it *and* help with dinner because Mom's got citizens' patrol tonight. By the time Camille slams the pasta and meatballs on the table, anything good about eating is over. Poppy has to work late—lucky her.

"I've had it, Mother, I feel like a slave. Mickey just sits around here doing *nothing* while I—"

"I'm doing stuff!"

"Right. You eat, sleep, and talk about *Joseph Alvarez*! I'm *sick* of hearing that man's name!"

Mom puts her fork down. "Camille, that's enough."

Camille shakes her head. "No. All he does is talk about Joseph Alvarez like he's . . . like he's . . . Dad come back or something!" Camille pushes away her dinner plate and starts crying. "I don't know why Daddy didn't send someone to look in on *me*!"

Mom reaches out to her. "Oh, honey."

"I try so hard not to think about Daddy. But sometimes I just need to have him here so bad. . . ."

Mom's staring straight ahead. "I understand."

We're all looking down at the table. I say I think Joseph Alvarez came for all of us.

Camille's standing now. "No he didn't. He doesn't care about me. He's helping you with pool and—"

"He'd help you with your game, Camille, if—"

"*I don't like pool! I don't like living in this town! I feel like I don't belong anywhere!*"

Mom gets her car keys and the big mega-flashlight the citizens' patrol uses. Camille starts running out of the dining room and Mom grabs her arm. "We're all going," she says. "Right now."

I've only ridden on patrol a few times. It's so cool. I'm in the front seat of the Chevy with Mom, feeling at least thirteen. Camille's in the back not talking. Mom's driving slowly down Flax Street, past the fix-it shop, Cassetti's Bakery. I'm watching hard for anything suspicious—open doors, trucks parked where they shouldn't be.

"Camille," Mom says, "I can't make you care for a place that I love. I wish I could. I don't even know if I can explain to you what this town means to me. I've lived so many places I didn't care about that finding one that was special was a gift. There isn't much in Cruckston that's pretty the way we think beauty should be. There isn't much here that distinguishes us from other places. We don't live above Vernon's because I'm still hanging on to the ghost of your father. We stay because the values that I hold dear in this world—loyalty, hard work, love,

125

determination—are here. And there's no better way I know to teach my children what I believe in and care about than to have us live in a place where they see these things happening around us every day.''

Mom turns left down Mariah. "I've never told either of you this—I could never count on my father. He'd go off places and come back weeks later than he said he would. He'd promise we'd go on vacations, promise he'd be there for us. He just couldn't stick around or didn't want to. It was awful for my mother. For a long time it was hard for me to trust people and feel secure.''

I look at Mom. I don't know what to say. I hold up my bad hand because it's beginning to ache.

Mom points to the apartments above the stores lining Mariah Boulevard. "When your father died, all these people poured out to comfort me. They didn't give me pat promises at the funeral. They didn't tell me that everything was going to be all right. They *stood* with me, they *cried* with me until it was all right. No one here is a fancy dresser, Camille, and the colors you love so much aren't in grand display, but if you can focus your eyes to look inside the hearts of these people, you will see a rainbow of colors. That's what I see. That's why I stay.''

Camille's crying soft in the backseat. "Mom, I'm so sorry. . . .''

Mom hands her a tissue. "I know.''

I turn to Camille and say there's no hard feelings. Camille nods and keeps crying.

Mom lets me shine the flashlight back and forth along the row of cars behind the fence at Zeke's

Towing. The light's so strong it shines anything bad out of hiding. A rat runs underneath the tow truck.

Mom picks up the cellular phone the phone company donated to the patrol and punches buttons.

"This is Ruth at the south end," she says into the receiver, turning past St. Xavier's onto Botts Street. "It's looking safe and sound from here."

The next morning I'm in my room lying on my lower bunk bed on the quilt that Mom dyed pool-room green to go with the pool-ball pillows Camille made for me. She dyed the curtains green, too, which Arlen says just multiplies the experience. I put my autograph collection of the pool greats of the world in my closet because I didn't want to look at it.

Joseph Alvarez just got back from Canada. I hear the Peterbilt and don't get up. I don't want him to see me like this.

I can hear him running up the stairs.

Hear him talking to Mom.

Hear his big boots clomping on the floor as he moves toward my room. He knocks on my door.

"It's open."

He walks in sad, looks at my splint. "Oh, son . . ."

"I'm sorry." I fight hard not to cry. "I can't play in the tournament!"

"You don't know that for sure now."

I start shouting that even if I can play, I can't play good enough to win because I can't practice for being an idiot!

Joseph Alvarez stands there holding his hat. "I'm so sorry, Mickey."

We don't say anything for the longest while.

Joseph Alvarez puts down his hat and starts talking about living in Mexico when he was a boy. His family was poor. His mother sold flowers on the street; his father drove a taxi. He said once some tourists were riding by his village on horses, going fast through the streets, and a girl fell off her horse, hurt bad. All the people in the village came out to help. The women brought water, the children brought cloth for bandages, the men lifted the girl gentle into an old truck and took her to the hospital, where the doctor fixed her up.

"See, we're all connected to each other," he says. "Some people you just know for an instant, others are for life. And when things get bad, like when we get hurt, we've got to let the people around us help."

I don't say anything.

"Have you been going in the hall?" he asks.

"No."

"You've got to start doing it, son, watching people play the game you'll be playing soon. Learn from their game, play them in your head. Everybody makes mistakes—I'm a living testimonial to that."

I'm standing now, shoving out my bandaged hand toward him. "The tournament's two weeks away! I'm not going to beat Buck! He'll be too old to compete next year. *I don't want to talk about it anymore!*"

Three days pass.

Nobody mentions my hand.

I'm sitting at the kitchen table eating Oreos when Poppy slaps her fist on the table.

"Listen up because I'm only going to say this once."

I'm about to tell her I've had a pretty hard day at school.

"People would pay a lot of money for the advice I'm about to give you, Mickey Vernon. I don't talk much about the arthritis I've got in my hands. I don't think complaining about things makes them any better. But my hands hurt every day. Sometimes I wonder if it's worth getting out of bed, but then I've got to go to the bathroom, and suddenly the trip seems worth it." She puts her hand on my shoulder. "You've just got to keep walking through it, honey. Don't run, don't hide, just walk. Eventually it's going to get better. It won't stay like this forever.''

She takes three Oreos from the bag and leaves me there.

Arlen and I are walking the long way back to my house from his house past Shankiss's Hole. We saw Buck and Pike Lorey hanging by Woolworth's and figured a detour was better than getting beat up. Other than people sitting on the pool tables and misusing the equipment, Shankiss's Hole gets Poppy, along with everyone else in town, the most upset about life.

I look past the DANGER signs around the fenced-off construction site and stare into the big hole in the ground. The bulldozers made it two years ago when Mr. Shankiss was going to build his restaurant and revitalize Flax Street until he ran out of money and just left it there as an eyesore four blocks from Vernon's and made himself the most hated man in all of Cruckston, New Jersey.

Quitter. That's what people call him. He could have made a difference and he quit. Quit on his responsibilities, quit on the people who were counting on him.

Quit on his dream.

I look down deep in Shankiss's Hole and feel my dream buried in the dirt. Arlen takes out his mechanical pencil, calculator, and a pad of paper from his bookbag. At least I helped him remember it today.

"I've been doing some figuring," he says, punching calculator buttons. "According to my calculations, you shouldn't be depressed."

"What?"

"Figuring," he says, "the average life span for an American male is about seventy-three, and given the fact that you are ten, you have lived out approximately one-eighth of your life, meaning you have about sixty-three years left to make good."

I sniff.

"If you were ancient, like in your forties, I'd say stay depressed, more than half your life is gone, there might not be another tournament. But at ten, Mickey, you're going to have a lot more opportunities to nail Buck and a ton of other guys." Arlen's punching buttons like crazy. "And," he says, "this three-week setback only represents less than one tenth of one percent of your life, assuming you're going to make seventy-three, but you could last longer. You could live to be one hundred, in which case, you're looking at six one hundredths of a percent, which is basically nothing in the whole sphere of the universe."

"My dad died young, Arlen!"

Arlen's calculating away and writing down numbers. "Even if you don't go as long as the averages, and you go a lot earlier, you're still talking small percentages. If I were you, I'd definitely feel better. The numbers don't lie."

Arlen puts the calculator back in his pocket. "We need to go to the hall," he says, and starts off down the street.

I stand there.

Arlen turns to me. "Are you going to argue with *math*?"

It's the first time I've set foot in Vernon's for ten days.

I love the echo the balls make when they jump in the pocket. I love the way the pool sticks hang on the wall like soldiers.

I love the way Buck misses easy shots when we make gasser noises at him. I stand at table twenty-one and roll the white cue ball across the empty table.

Take it slow.

Arlen is holding the mechanical bridge—that's an extender for a pool stick—and I'm shooting one-handed. I'm going to use whatever I can to make my game better.

A siren's blaring in the distance. Buck's kissing his stick and dancing with it in the corner.

I look away and concentrate. I miss a lot of shots at first. It's frustrating. But slowly I get the hang of playing one-handed.

I line up the shot and tap. Three in the side. Not perfect, but not bad.

Arlen stays for dinner so we can work on our science fair project. Mom is at night school, Camille is at the dress rehearsal for her play. Poppy makes us macaroni and cheese, which her mother used to make for her when she was pushing on a homework assignment. Poppy says her mother's macaroni and cheese has special brain-enlarging calories that have never failed her yet, which is why she's such an intelligent fireball to this day.

We're leaning over the dining room table; Arlen just finished drawing the sheet that shows about angles—the angles the ball makes off the rail, and the angles where the cue ball hits the object ball.

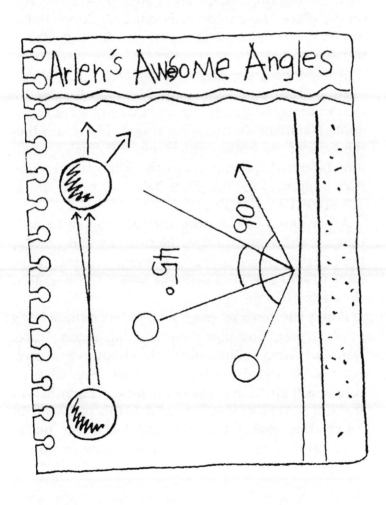

I say pool is cooler than volcanoes.

"If we just had something that *explodes*," Arlen says.

We walk down the long hall to the living room and find the creakiest place in our floor. If you step just right it makes a creepy wailing sound: *Weeeeeeeaaaaaaaaaccccchhhhh.* When Camille has her friend Olivia over, Arlen and I rock back and forth on the place and creep Olivia out bad. Poppy put a little hooked rug over the spot, but that just makes it easier to find.

Weeeeeeeeeaaaaaaaaaacccccccccchhhhhhh.

We go into the living room. Mom's palm tree by the window is dying. Poppy says we don't get enough sunlight in the living room. All the sun hits the back of the house, which is why Poppy's geraniums bloom three seasons in the kitchen. Sunlight isn't a big deal for me. Pool halls stay pretty much the same, day or night.

Arlen and I are waiting for his mother to pick him up and I put on the video of my dad playing pool. Arlen never minds watching it. I put it on once when Petie Pencastle was here and he wanted to watch cartoons.

Poppy sits down to watch with us, even though it's hard for her. The tape's choppy, but I don't care. Dad's wearing a blue shirt. He shoots some awesome shots and the video cuts to me as a baby, sitting in a high chair picking my nose. "Eight ball in the side," Dad says to me, and I stop picking and watch. Dad makes the shot and I clap my pudgy little hands. I'm just watching the memories I don't remember spill out. Poppy wipes away a tear. Dad's bending over the table, shooting ball after ball.

Bam.

Pow.

In they go.

"He said he could sometimes see a line going from the cue ball through the object ball right into the pocket," Poppy says softly.

Arlen and I sit up. "What kind of line?" we say together.

"I don't know. He said it was like a line showing him the way."

Arlen looks up to heaven and closes his eyes. He does this when he's getting math ideas. He gets out graph paper and starts drawing a pool table and a ball with lines shooting through it. His mother comes to the front door, which doesn't interest him much.

"He had an idea," I tell Mrs. Pepper.

She plops down. "We could be here all night."

Arlen's drawing like mad, measuring lines, drawing angles. "This," he declares, "is unbelievable!"

"Arlen," pleads his mother, "math will wait. Your father will not. We have to go!"

Arlen turns toward his mother. "Mom, do you know what Galileo said?"

Arlen's bringing out the big guns. Galileo is a dead scientist who used math a lot. He's one of Arlen's heroes. Arlen puts his hand over his heart.

"Galileo said, 'The universe stands continually open to our gaze, but it cannot be understood unless one first learns to comprehend the language and interpret the characters in which it is written. It is written in the language of mathematics, and its characters are triangles, circles, and other geometrical figures, without which it is humanly impossible to understand a single word of it; without these, one is wandering about in a dark labyrinth.'"

A labyrinth is like a maze. Arlen has this quotation on the Galileo poster in his room.

"Fifteen minutes," says Mrs. Pepper, and takes out her knitting. She's making a pink sweater.

Arlen draws a ball on a piece of paper and another ball with a line through it heading for a pocket.

"A vector," he says, "is a line that takes you from

one place to the next. That means your father was using vectors to make his shots. He could see the lines going from the balls to the pockets like they were drawn on the table. He didn't have math as a language so he couldn't tell it to anyone else. His language was his stick. He could only show it."

My heart's pounding.

Arlen turns to Poppy. "Can you remember anything more that Mr. Vernon said about seeing the line?"

Poppy's thinking. "He just said it kind of shot through his eye, went through the cue ball, and he could see the table and what he was supposed to do."

"See the table," Arlen repeated.

"That's what he said."

"See the table!" Arlen shouts. "Have you ever seen those lines when you shoot, Mickey?"

"No, I can do the angles, but—"

"I need string!" Arlen yells.

Mrs. Pepper holds up her pink yarn.

"Yes, yarn is perfect!" Arlen shouts. "We have to go downstairs! We have to see the table!"

Arlen's just scattered nine balls on table eight and is cutting the pink yarn in pieces. He lays a piece of yarn from each ball to its closest pocket until table eight looks like a diagram.

"I think that's how your father saw it, except the lines weren't pink." He makes a face.

I look at the table. It's one of those simple answers you don't think about.

"But each time a ball moves the lines will be different," I say.

"You've got to train your mind to see them," says Arlen. "Your dad did it naturally."

"And then there's English," I say. "You've got to be able to hit the balls just right to line up your next shot."

"Geometry doesn't explain the way you have to hit the ball," Arlen explains. "That's calculus."

"As I live and breathe," says Poppy, "I think this will work."

I think if Poppy hadn't seen it for herself she wouldn't have talked Mom into letting me stay up late and try the experiment. Mrs. Pepper drags Arlen halfway home and then they come back to get his jacket.

"This shouldn't count!" Arlen pleads to his mother as he retrieves his coat. "I was helping a friend in need! Be merciful!"

He throws me another drawing.

The pink yarn is junking up the table, so I have to take it off, brush the matt, and use string instead. I cut different lengths, placing them on the table. Then I memorize the line that goes from the ball into the pocket and try the shot using the bridge.

I make most of the shots.

Poppy tries some, too. "Well, I'll be!" she shouts.

I want to tear the bandage off my hand and start playing for real.

My left hand's doing good.

Mom makes me go to bed. I curl up in my green

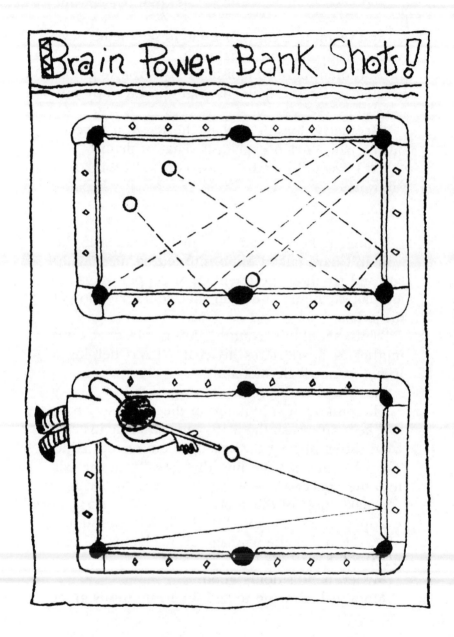

quilt and listen to the *click, click* of pool balls in the hall below. I study Arlen's drawing and put it under my pillow. I close my eyes and try to imagine table eight in a big geometric pattern—the balls lying there, breaking apart, moving, and those lines going right through the balls, into the pockets, and slamming through Buck Pender's dirty rotten heart.

In school I keep seeing the table. Long shots. Short shots. Bank shots. Vectors.

I'm seeing geometry everywhere—diamond-shaped ball fields, birds flying in V formation. I have grapes for lunch and think about circles. Then I ram the grapes across my tray with my straw.

Wham.

Two grapes in the corner.

It's all connected.

Mrs. Riggles gives us extra time to work on our soldier letters, which are due tomorrow. Arlen and I are in our favorite corner in the school library, sitting in the soft brown chairs, tucked behind the science fiction section. I just finished my letter.

Dear Mother and Father,

I am writing to let you know how I am. Things are not as good as I would like them to be. I was shot in the arm and my arm is in a sling, but the good news is that it is feeling okay now, although I will be awhile getting back to battle. It was frightening to be shot. I did something stupid near the battle line and a Redcoat got me, but my friends pulled me away and saved my life.

I guess you know by now that we lost the Battle of Germantown and the British took Philadelphia. We feel so bad that we couldn't hold on. Retreating from that battle was the hardest thing I've ever had to do. I felt like we were letting everyone down.

When I think of my comfortable home and warm bed and all the good food you supply, it's hard for me to believe what has happened to us at Valley Forge. The conditions are so hard. We've had to cut down trees to make huts and burn wood for fires. There's nothing left here now to break the wind. We are cold and hungry. We are tired and sick. I'm told we came here last month with 12,000 men, but there won't be that many when we leave.

There is no medicine, so my arm must get better on its own. There is not much hope, either. The most hope we see comes from General George Washington. He is the finest man I have ever known. He reminds us every day that our cause is good. I trust him to do the right thing. I think he would make a great president someday (hint, hint).

Other than that, I am doing all right. I have a torn blanket to keep me warm. I'm real lucky to have it, too. Not everyone has this much. If I get back home, I will never take anything for granted again.

Your son,
John
Lieutenant John Q. Milner
Valley Forge, Pennsylvania
January 11, 1778

Arlen finished his letter too. He had to use his calculator. He figured how many potatoes, barrels of sauerkraut, and pounds of meat each man needed to survive for three months plus how many wagons it would take to deliver the supplies. The sauerkraut had loads of vitamin C to help fight diseases like scurvy. Arlen decided that his soldier came from a rich, brave farming family who could bring the food to Valley Forge and change the course of history. Arlen said his letter would probably get his soldier promoted from private first class to at least master sergeant.

My doctor's appointment is tomorrow.

It's the last period of the day at school. Mrs. Riggles is standing in front of the blackboard. "What," she asks the class, "is the bravest thing you've ever done?"

We all look at each other.

Sally Stoletto says calling 911 when her grandmother had a stroke and helping her breathe until the ambulance came.

Arlen says taking Mangler to the animal hospital without any money in a cab after he'd been hit by that motorcycle.

"Were either of you frightened?"

"Yeah!" Arlen and Sally say together.

"Courage," Mrs. Riggles says, "rarely comes without fear. Courage rises above fear and makes people more than they think they can be."

She holds up a picture of Paul Revere riding his horse. "Let's talk about the acts of courage during the Revolutionary War."

I take out my history book and feel something shoot through me, like I'm connected to all the acts of courage in the whole world.

Whether I get to the finals or choke in the early rounds, I know what I have to do.

CHAPTER

"Does that hurt?"

Dr. Oglethorpe is pushing around my left wrist.

"No."

"How about that?" She's watching me hard. It hurts.

"No."

She bends it up.

"Ouch!"

Dr. Oglethorpe takes a deep breath and steps back.

"It's been three weeks," I tell her. "The swelling's gone. You said I'd be okay in three weeks."

"I said we'd see. When is this tournament?" she asks.

"A week. And I've got to play!"

"Mickey!" says Mom.

"And I've got to practice, too! Every day!"

"Make a fist," Dr. Oglethorpe says. I make a

strong one. She folds her arms and looks at me. "Well, I suppose if Mickey Mantle could play baseball for nineteen seasons of unceasing pain, Mickey Vernon can play this week. You can't do any permanent damage."

Yes!

Mom's looking worried.

"But," the doctor says, "you use ice regularly, you take Tylenol every six hours, you listen to what your body is telling you, Mickey. If it hurts too much, you stop and rest and put your splint back on. Deal?"

"Deal."

"One more thing," says the doctor. "Just how good are you on a pool table?"

"I'm okay," I say.

"He's awesome," says Mom.

I get my rack of balls and walk to table twelve, cool, like Joseph Alvarez does. I've got catching up to do. I walk by Buck, who's nailing shots on table six.

"You get the diaper off your hand, *Vernon?*"

I look right past him.

"Excellent," Arlen whispers. "Pay no attention. He's a dead man. Total concentration. We're here for one thing."

Arlen racks the balls. I take a stick from the wall, feel its weight. I take some practice strokes at the air. It's good to be back.

I bend over table twelve.

Aim at the racked balls dead center.

And on the *snap.*

The balls go flying, but nothing drops. I rub my left wrist. It aches. But I expected that. No pain, no gain. I aim again and shoot the one ball. The two. Arlen asks if I need ice yet.

No.

I need to practice. I need to catch up.

Pow.

Arlen's using string and a ruler to show the lines the balls will travel. "You've got to think about the lines the other balls will follow when you pick your shots." He takes the string away. "Can you see it?"

"Not yet."

I'm rubbing my wrist. My fingers hurt. "Line up the shot," Arlen says, "see the line the ball will travel, find the angle of incidence, and hit it *there.*"

I'm playing for position.

Hit the four with English, let the cue ball move into place near the five. I scratch on the six. I wasn't thinking ahead.

Joseph Alvarez comes in to watch me.

Arlen and I show him all about seeing the table. He says that in all the years he'd known my dad he never told him about the lines. He really gets into it, and we're all brainstorming together about different shots and the lines Dad might have seen cutting through them. That's when he tells me to just call him Joseph if I want, which I really do.

"Welcome back," Joseph says, and puts a thin gray case on table twelve. "Open it."

I open it. There's a cue stick inside. White and gray with black racing stripes.

I look at him.

"That's a decent stick for you," he says. "It'll fit your hands and weight."

I'm looking at the stick. *My own* stick—a Meucci. I don't know what to say.

He screws it together for me. I take it. The weight is perfect.

"It's great, Joseph! Man!" I'm aiming it. Arlen's touching it like it's made of diamonds. *"Thank you!"*

"My pleasure, son. You earned it."

I take a few shots with it; a few more. The light on table twelve beams over us. It's like the stick was made for me.

But my hand's hurting bad. I promised Mom I wouldn't push it. I look over at Buck, who's crashing balls into pockets like a machine, and go upstairs with Joseph to ice my hand.

I keep ice on it up to when we leave for Cruckston High School to see Camille's play. Nobody told me it was about people falling in love. I close my eyes every time the boy and girl get close and start singing. The costumes are almost the best part. The best part is when the curtain crashes down on one of the dancer's heads right when she's twirling and everyone onstage is shouting to pull it back up.

Camille goes onstage at the end and everyone claps for her. I stomp my feet up and down so I won't hurt my hand, and make a much cooler noise than clapping.

Six days to go.

All day at school I keep thinking about the tournament.

During recess, when we're playing king of the mountain and I keep getting shoved off too easy when I make it to the top.

During art, while I'm working on my African warrior mask, painting the papier-mâché cheeks bright gold and purple. I stick feathers at the top and make the mouth look angry and I picture this huge warrior with a spear doing a death dance around Buck Pender. T. R. Dobbs is working on his mask next to me. He's descended from African Zulu warriors and he says a Zulu never retreats in the face of the enemy. I'm descended mostly from potato farmers, which isn't a lot to hold on to when you need to be tough. I lift the mask to my face and shout the Zulu war cry T.R. taught me.

"Zuuuu*luuuu* Zuuuu*luuuu!*"

Mr. Pez, the art teacher, looks up. I look down and keep painting. Nobody turns me in.

It's easy to be brave when the enemy isn't around.

The days go fast and slow. I keep practicing and my hand keeps hurting.

I'm wondering how athletes play in pain. Arlen said it must be the big-time money they earn that keeps them going. I'm playing anyway, but playing's like a blur.

Hitting.

Breaking.

Over and over.

Arlen hasn't left anything anywhere for six whole days. He has his motto, THINK WOOD, everywhere.

I'm thinking wood now too, and really helping him. Every time I pick up my new stick I make him check his stuff to see if he forgot anything. Best friends help each other.

Mom's worried. She says I'm too driven. She yelled at Joseph when he was telling me the great secret of the pros—play your best, whether you're ahead or behind.

"Is that all that's important to you?" she shouted. *"Winning?"*

"No, Ruthie, it's just something to shoot for."

I'm definitely behind.

The days click off. It's hard to concentrate in school. Mrs. Riggles calls Mom in for a conference about it and Mom gets all upset at me, even though I got an A minus on my soldier letter. Mom says the tournament is becoming bigger than life.

"It's always been pretty big," I say.

"I want you to *concentrate* on your schoolwork!"

Mrs. Riggles is so worked up about the American Revolution, she's jumping to 1783, when the Treaty of Paris was signed and the British and the Americans finally quit fighting; jumping back to 1775 and Paul Revere's ride, when he warned the colonists that the Redcoats were coming. Mrs. Riggles teaches history backward and forward so we'll get the connections. She says Paul Revere had to push beyond himself and his personal safety to get on that horse and sound the warning to his countrymen.

I'm looking at the picture of Paul Revere on Mrs. Riggles's desk wondering how he found the courage.

* * *

We have pasta for dinner Friday night. I have thirds to boost my energy for the next day. The tournament starts in thirteen hours.

I'm watching a video of my dad playing pool. It's the only video we've got when he loses.

Dad's wearing a green shirt and black pants. The sign behind him says WORLD CLASS BILLIARDS. The crowd watching him is quiet out of respect. Dad's in stroke, shooting fast and easy, holding his stick like it's part of his arm. His body curves into the slam he gets on the ball. He's smiling.

Then he messes up. Hits a bummer shot, which leaves him with nothing. The crowd groans. Dad's face gets hard. He tries a tough bank shot on the seven ball and misses bad. The crowd sighs, but Dad just shrugs, smiles, and steps away from the table as the guy he's playing wins the championship.

The crowd is clapping away. Dad's the first one up to shake the winner's hand. He's still smiling and it's for real, not those fake smiles losers get sometimes. He slaps that man on the shoulder and whispers something in the guy's ear. The guy laughs and Dad walks off to let the winner have his day.

I think about that as I brush my teeth and get into bed.

I know my dad wanted to win that tournament, but losing didn't crush him. Maybe losing can only hurt you if you open the door and let it in.

Poppy comes into my room with an ice pack.

151

"I don't think I'm going to do too well tomorrow," I say, getting used to the idea.

Poppy sits on the bed next to me and puts the ice pack on my hand. "Only the good Lord knows what's going to happen, honey. But I can tell you this—sometimes just standing tall is a whale of a victory."

CHAPTER

20

This is it.

Kids are everywhere.

Banners are flying.

Parents are giving last-minute playing tips, waving their arms and shouting that it's only a *game*.

Mrs. Cassetti keeps running across the street from the bakery asking if anything's happened yet. Mr. Kopchnik closed his store for the day to root for me. Mr. Gatto's here too. He got his son-in-law Dolan to manage Cut Rate Gas and Groceries, even though he says Dolan might run the business into the ground before lunch. Camille walks by with Brad Lunder, her almost boyfriend; she messes up my hair, wishes me extra good luck, and says that now that my splint is off, I can go back to *laundry*.

I'm standing at table nine putting my stick together. I'm wearing my black T-shirt, khakis, and my new high-top Nikes with super-mega-traction. My first game is with Rick Plotsky, who's a pretty good player.

"Don't be nervous."

It's Francine. She sits on a folding chair. She's wearing an orange neon sweatshirt that says I BELIEVE IN MAGIC. "Nervous is a dirty word, Mickey. Nervous is out of your vocabulary." She lowers her voice. "I lit a candle for you this morning at Mass."

"Thanks."

Francine whips a magic red scarf from her sleeve as Arlen runs up, adjusts his glasses, and looks at me.

"You're ready," he says.

"Yeah."

Buck pushes through the crowd, growling. His father marches behind him; Mr. Pender's got a purplish splotch running down the side of his face. His eyes are puffy and gray. Mrs. Pender runs to catch up with them. She's fiddling with her wedding ring, nervous.

"Well, this is nice," she says to Buck, who doesn't answer her.

Buck stares at Jerry Docks, who he's playing first. Jerry gets pale.

Mom's clutching her necklace, asking me about my hand for the third time.

"It's fine," I say, which is half true.

She looks at Serena and smiles brave as Joseph pats me on the back. "Play with heart, son. That's all you need to bring to the table."

154

Big Earl is checking in the last-minute sign-ups. I rub my left hand, which I've been icing since I got up. It's near frozen.

"I'm sorry! It wasn't my fault!"

Petie Pencastle is standing in front of me, waving his arms.

"Huh?"

"I told my parents it wouldn't be fair; he's *so big* and all and nobody was expecting him!"

Petie points a shaky finger toward the counter, where a huge boy is signing the tournament sheet. "It's my cousin!" Petie wails. "They're up visiting from Elizabeth for the weekend. He's a real good player, Mickey." Petie lowers his voice. "They call him the *Sledgehammer.*"

We look at the giant, who's getting instructions from Big Earl. If Arlen and I stood side by side, we'd maybe be as wide.

"He's too old to play!" Arlen shouts. "You can't play if you're over thirteen. He's sixteen at least."

"He's thirteen," Petie says, groaning. "He turns fourteen next week. His father had to show his birth certificate at school. He's too big to fit into the desks. They must be giving him steroids."

"This isn't happening!" Arlen screams.

I look at Buck, who's doing his shoulder-loosening motion.

I look at the Sledgehammer, who's so big he's casting a shadow over the counter.

I put both hands on table nine and lean over.

I'm finished.

Joseph Alvarez leans in. "Blinders," he says.

Man. It's so much easier when you're practicing.

Poppy blows her tournament whistle. I move slowly into place.

Poppy runs her kids' tournament official, just like the grown-up ones.

"We're going to play this tournament like the great game of pool should be played," Poppy shouts to the crowd. She's wearing her red Vernon's sweatshirt today—Poppy always wears red on special occasions. "We don't want any foul language. We don't want any cheating. If you do either of these things, you're out."

Slam. Poppy's fist hits the counter.

"We've got umpires at each table and, believe me, you don't want to mess with them."

All the umps look tough—Snake Mensker, Big Earl Reed. Madman Turcell shakes his ponytail like a crazy dog and cracks his knuckles.

"Now let's face the flag of our great land and say the Pledge of Allegiance."

Poppy brings the flag out for tournaments. I'm saying the pledge loud like I've been taught. Buck's not pledging and I wonder if I can turn him in.

"All right now!" Poppy screams.

The kids who won first up bend down to break.

The umpires lean forward.

Poppy blows her whistle. *"Crack 'em good!"*

There's a crash so loud it shakes the walls as twenty-four cue balls ram across twenty-four tables.

My heart's pumping.

Pool games are won one ball at a time.

Rick Plotsky gets nothing in on the break.

My turn. I make the one, two, three. I miss the
four, but Rick does too. We battle ball for ball, but I
win.

"Game to Mickey Vernon," says Madman, punching the air.

I win the second game too. It's best two out of
three.

"And that's a match to Mickey Vernon."

Rick and I shake hands.

"Good game," I tell him, and win first up against
T. R. Dobbs, who just won his match. T.R. has never
beat me.

I dig down deep and break with my whole body.
The cue ball rams the one clean and breaks the
balls apart. Six in the back corner. I chalk my stick
light, moving around the table. No good shots. I do
a safety like Joseph showed me—hiding the cue ball
behind another ball to give your opponent a hard
shot.

T.R. groans at the nightmare I left him and tries
shooting the one, but gets the nine ball in by mistake. That's the worst thing you can do.

"Game to Mickey Vernon," says Madman.

I do like the way that sounds.

I ace the next rack. My match again.

My hand's hurting, but I don't care.

Dinah Glossup and I are up next. She's a tough
player. We battle hard. She snookers me behind the
eight ball—I can't get a clear shot on the six and
flub the shot bad. Dinah wins the first game. I blow
two shots on the rail. I just win the second game.

I look over at Buck, who is definitely gunning

down the enemy on table three. Pike Lorey is shouting every time Buck makes a shot. Poppy tells Pike if he doesn't zip that lip of his, she's going to pick four of her biggest umpires to toss him in the street.

Pike shuts up, fuming.

I'm taking Tylenol for my third game with Dinah. I break hard. Eight in the corner.

English on the one to gain position, look at the effect each shot will have on the next. Find the angles.

Shoot it straight.

Concentrate.

I win it.

Dinah shakes my hand.

I'm looking around. I don't know where Arlen is.

I'm rubbing talcum powder on my hands so my stick won't slip. I win three more matches, four.

"Match to Mickey Vernon." Madman's saying it over and over.

We stop for lunch. I'm icing my hand. It's aching bad. I haven't played this long since I sprained it. I'm taking deep breaths, keeping my focus. Easy stroke. Easy win.

I find Arlen in the corner by the Sledgehammer's table writing something on a piece of paper. He always watches *me* play. I tell him I've been winning.

"Well, *of course* you have," he says, and goes back to writing.

Poppy comes over, looks at my left wrist.

"How bad is it?" she asks. "You tell me the truth now."

"It's half bad." The soreness is shooting from

158

my wrist through my fingers. My elbow's feeling it too.

"Can you play?"

"I can play."

"Then don't concentrate on where it hurts. Concentrate on all the places that feel fine."

"Is that what you do?"

"Every day."

Poppy blows her whistle and we're playing again. My nose is feeling pretty good and I concentrate on that. I'm shooting, breaking, banking, hurting.

The games blur into each other. Straight shots. Safeties. Double banks. I'm acing my banks.

Ninety-degree angles.

Forty-fives.

Divide the angle by two. Nail it hard and *yes*.

I make a 140-degree bank against Shelty Zoller and Madman's eyes go back in his head.

I'm still standing.

I'm playing twelve- and thirteen-year-olds now. Nicky Prinz. Ted Carothers. Pike Lorey. Pike tries cheating and moving the cue ball, saying he didn't mean to touch it. Madman is all over him and gives me the game. I whip Pike extra nice on the second rack, just in case he didn't think I could lick him for real.

But with each new game, my hand gets worse. Still, the Meucci's shooting like a rifle.

I don't know where it's coming from.

Madman's saying it different each time.

"*Match* to Mickey Vernon."

"Match *to* Mr. Vernon."

159

"And another match to *Mick the Stick!*"

Mom is grinning.

Joseph Alvarez is beaming.

Poppy's playing it cool, but I can tell inside she's busting.

Where is Arlen?

It's three o'clock.

I keep climbing higher, higher, one ball at a time. I've got to play Tim Irons. He's a monster on position. Tim gets in place. I'm looking over at Arlen but he's watching the Sledgehammer like he's the big show.

What's he doing?

I've got to focus. Blinders like my dad. Tim's big. He's got power. He's not injured.

He throws himself into the break, cracks the balls apart, but gets nothing in.

But what he leaves me is a miracle. An easy shot off the one ball to pocket the nine. If I make it, I win the game with one shot.

I make it.

Anything can happen in nine ball.

"Game to Mickey here!" Madman shouts.

I can't believe it.

Tim slumps over as Madman racks the balls.

My break. I bust them up—three ball in the corner. I foul on the one and Tim uses it for position. We battle to the wire until the nine ball's left. Tim makes it, but he scratches on the break in the next game. I don't know how, but the balls roll with me. I run the table, tap the nine in the side. Tim's standing there like he's been struck by lightning.

"Maaaaaaaaaaaatch to Mickey Vernon."
Yes!

It's four o'clock.

There are four players left. Me, Buck, Cindy Gras-sini, and the Sledgehammer. I'm the only player not thirteen years old. It's a miracle I'm here. I stand extra tall because I'm the shortest.

My hand is throbbing. I don't know if I can play anymore.

Poppy puts our names in a Yankees cap and picks two at a time to decide who'll play who next. Cindy is the only one I can maybe beat, and I'm not laying money on it. She's tough. Poppy hands the names to the umpires. I'm trying to read her face, but she's wearing the one she uses for poker—eyes straight ahead, jaw shut, the one Big Earl says no one can decipher.

"How come I gotta go there?" Buck Pender's looking at Snake Mensker, who's pointing over at my table.

"Because I said so."

I close my eyes.

No!

I got *Buck!*

That's it.

I'm not going to even make the finals. This whole year I've been picturing Buck and me as the last guys standing.

Snake steps back to let Buck pass. Mr. and Mrs. Pender follow him. Mrs. Pender whispers, "Be a good sport now, Buck." Cindy Grassini walks to the Sledgehammer's table.

My hand hurts so bad. I stand there at table nine because I don't know what else to do.

Buck stomps over, wipes his mouth on his workshirt, and looks at me, laughing.

"You're going down, *Vernon*."

"This is the semifinal round!" Poppy announces.

The pool hall is quieter than I've ever heard it. I step up to the table; I've got the break.

Mom has her arms folded tight, trying not to look nervous.

Joseph Alvarez nods at me and winks.

The crowd around the table is two deep. Buck's people on the left, mine on the right. I can't concentrate on who's here. I can't think about my hand and how much it hurts. I can't worry that Buck's trying to get to me with that expression on his face that says I'm wasting his time.

This is the semifinals.

Slam.

I ram my stick into the white cue ball and get two in on the break. My people applaud extra loud.

I make the one. The three. Just get the five, tip

the six into the corner pretty wobbly, but it goes in. That's all that matters in pool. Three balls left.

I can't look at Buck even though he's looking at me. I can feel it, though. Feel his fat smile breaking across his face.

I miss the seven.

Stupid!

My people groan.

Buck steps up to the table like he owns it. He looks at his father, who doesn't look back. Buck aims long on the seven, bends down, and rams it straight in.

He eyeballs the eight. It's lying on the rail—a tough shot. Buck wipes sweat from his forehead, wipes sweat from his hands. He aims low; his stick slips.

The eight moves three inches.

I hit it in fast and set up pretty for the nine ball. I get the nine nice in the side pocket.

"Yes!" shouts Joseph above the rest.

"Match to Mr. Mickey Vernon!" Madman shouts, strutting.

Buck's looking at me like he can't believe it.

I look right back at him.

Believe it.

Madman racks the balls. I've got maybe one more break in me and then my hand's going to stop working. I push back on my super-mega-traction Nikes.

The cue ball crashes down the table.

Seven in the corner.

I rub my wrist. It hurts so bad. I do an okay safety on the one.

"I'll get him now," Buck says to his father. Mr. Pender sits there like a statue. The only thing moving is that vein beating in his neck. Mrs. Pender is fiddling with her purse strap.

Buck gets the one in the side in a great shot. He nails the two, the three, then he scratches on the four, which is a big mistake.

I put the cue ball by the four ball, which is three inches from the side pocket.

You can't beat me, *Vernon*.

Yes I can.

Wham!

My stick's on fire. Five in the corner. Bank the six in the side. Long drive on the eight—right on the money.

Just the nine ball and me.

Nobody's moving.

It's a long corner shot.

I look down the table like it's a runway. Focus in. Shoot.

And *yes!* The nine speeds into the corner. That's the *match!*

Mr. Kopchnik's shaking Mr. Gatto. "Did you see that, Gatto?"

"I saw it, Kopchnik!"

I touch the dark green cloth of table nine and throw back my head.

Madman yells it so everyone can hear. *"That's a shutout for Mickey Vernon!"*

I go toward Buck to shake hands, but he won't do it. He's yelling it's not fair, table nine's a bad table, his stick wasn't straight, the whole thing was rigged. He wants a rematch!

Mr. Pender's whole face is purple. He's shoving Buck toward the door. "How come you can't just lose *decent?*" he shouts.

Mrs. Pender stands there waving her skinny hands in the air like a little bird. "You did very well," she says to me. "You're a fine young man. I'm sorry about . . . my son. He . . . doesn't have much faith in himself."

She shakes my hand as the crowd breaks in on us like a big wave—Mom and Joseph and Camille and Poppy and Francine and Petie and T.R. and so many others. They're saying I did it and I looked tough. Buck's already gone. I can't believe I beat him. I look through the crowd to Arlen, who sticks his thumb up in the air and smiles at me and goes back to writing like mad.

Guys are slapping me on the back saying go give the big guy what for. I tell them thanks, I'll try. I don't have to pinch myself to see if I'm dreaming because my hand hurts too much. I know this is real.

I walk to the Sledgehammer, who won his match against Cindy.

"He's murder," Cindy says to me, moving off.

I don't know how I'm going to play.

I'm icing my hand.

Trying to find power in the fingers.

"I'm stopping this game, Mickey!" Mom shouts. "I will not let it be destructive to your body!"

"Mom, I've got to play."

"*No* you don't!"

I throw the ice pack down and grab her arm.

"I've got to!"

Joseph comes over. "Ruthie, I don't mean to interfere here, but a man's got to do what a man's got to do."

She spins around. "This isn't the streets of Laredo, Joseph! This is New Jersey! I can see the pain all over his face!"

I blow up my cheeks big to get the pain off. I don't think it works. I swallow hard. "It hurts, Mom. You're right. The doctor said I couldn't do any permanent damage. I've got to play."

Please.

She sits down on the bench against the wall underneath the photograph of Allen Hopkins, who was New Jersey state nine-ball champion four times and won the U.S. Open for nine ball twice.

"Okay," she whispers.

Joseph sits next to her and says something I can't hear. Mom shakes her head and smiles a little. He pats her on the hand. Arlen runs up to me and hands me a sheet of paper.

"He doesn't know the math, Mickey! Look, I've got it right here. I've watched every game the Sledgehammer's played *all day*. I've charted the shots he can make and the ones he can't in his last fifteen games. I know his patterns!"

"That's what you were doing?"

"What did you think I was doing?"

What a friend.

I look at the paper.

"Bad news first," Arlen says. "He has an awesome break and he's great on long straight shots—he made thirty out of thirty-five attempts. He's a power shooter. But he's got no touch when the balls are on the rail. See? He made three out of the last seventeen is all—that's only eighteen percent. Banks aren't much better. He made four out of the last sixteen tries for only twenty-five percent completion. He hasn't even tried a bank in the last six games! Every time he misses a bank or a rail shot, he gets upset and plays his next inning bad. I didn't clock his medium and short shots."

I check the stats.

The Sledgehammer's Scorecard

GAMES	BALLS IN ON BREAK	LONG STRAIGHT SHOTS	BANK SHOTS	ON THE RAIL SHOTS	COMBINATION SHOTS
1	NB	1-0-1-1	0-0	0-0-1	1-1
2	3	1-1-1-1	1-0	0-0	
3	1	1	0-0		O
4	1	1-1	O	0-0	
5	2	0-1-1-1	1	O	
6	NB	1-1	O	0-0	1-0-1
7	1	1-1	1-0	1-0	
8	2	O	0-0	1	O
9	1	1-1-1	1-0-0	O	
10	NB	1-1-0		O	1
11	2	1			O
12	1	1-0		O	
13	NB	1			
14	2	1-1-1		O	1
15	2	1-1			
Tries	11	35	16	17	10
Balls made	17	30	4	3	6
%	154%	86%	25%	18%	60%

$\left(= \dfrac{balls}{Tries} \times 100\right)$

NB = Not This Break
O = Tried and Failed

"You leave him bank and rail shots," Arlen is saying. "It's not the easiest thing, but try."

Joseph looks at the papers and slaps Arlen on the back. "Play position," Joseph says to me. "Don't look at his size. He's a big guy with weak points. Play them if you can. You control the ball."

"This is for the championship!" Poppy yells.

The Sledgehammer moves forward like a tank.

I take my stick in my good hand and walk to table two.

"You boys go at this clean, now," Poppy says.

The Sledgehammer and I shake hands; mine disappears inside his. My head comes more than halfway up his chest. He's got a mustard stain on the right shoulder of his striped shirt.

He smiles at me. "Good luck, kid."

I swallow big. "You too."

I get the break. I ram it with all I've got.

Six in the corner.

I make the one, the two. The three's impossible. I do a safety right on the rail. The Sledgehammer bends over the table and blows the rail shot bad just like Arlen said.

I make the three, miss the bank on the four, but I get lucky and leave him another bank. He shakes his head, bends over to shoot. He's sweating good. He looks around, goes for a safety.

Arlen was right!

My turn. I rub my hand.

I maneuver out of the safety and get lucky. I leave him another bank.

He blows it again.

I get a bead on the four and line it up. It zooms into the side pocket. I'm eyeballing the five. Smack. In it goes. Three more left. I get them too. Seven, eight, and nine.

"Game to Mickey Vernon!"

The crowd is applauding. Earl racks the balls.

Arlen's going, "Yes, *yes!*"

It's my break and my hand feels broken. I feel like crying, but I can't do that. I step back on my super-mega-traction Nikes and *whack.*

The crowd groans.

I can't believe it. The cue ball just nicks the one and sits there—nothing in—a total dud.

The Sledgehammer walks up smiling to take his inning. He's got shark teeth. He throws his huge body into the stroke.

He breaks the balls apart like lightning. The three ball zooms into the corner.

He hits the one, the two. He's eyeballing the four. Makes it in a combo off the eight. Gets a big round of applause. The five goes down, the six. The balls are lying perfect for him. He's running the table, picking off the seven, the eight in his long straight rifle shots. It's happening so fast.

He makes the nine easy.

"Game to Gordon Sledge," says Big Earl.

The Sledgehammer nods to the applauding crowd. Joseph slaps me on the shoulder as Earl racks the balls. The tank's break. If he runs them again, I'm history.

The balls crack apart like thunder. Seven in the corner.

The two's lying on the rail. I hold my breath.

He misses.

I let out a big breath, chalk my stick, and move toward the two ball.

I'm pushing out the crowd in my mind, pushing out the pain. I can't see the table like my dad, but I feel something. I smile big. And suddenly I see the lines. Not actual lines on the table, but I know where they'd be. I can feel where they'd be!

Shooting out from the balls, shooting out from my eyes. Shooting out from my stick like vectors straight and true right into the pockets, and not stopping there, continuing like lines do out the door, down the street, all the way to the New Jersey Turnpike, and clear down to Florida.

Energy zooms through my legs. Pool games are won one ball at a time. The energy carries me forward. It's stronger than the pain.

Two ball in the side. I bank around the five ball and get the three in the corner.

The crowd's going crazy.

Four ball in the side, five. Bring the cue ball back for position on the six. Control the ball. Don't concentrate on where it hurts. Feel the winning pump through my blood.

I bank the six clean, bring the cue ball around to the eight. Give it a nice tap with the bridge and *miss*!

No!

I push back from the table feeling dead as Gordon Sledge takes his inning. He taps the eight in. Only the nine ball's left—a hard slice shot. If he makes it, he's got the game. I think he's going to make it.

The Sledgehammer's sweating.

He wipes his wide face.

Just do it!

He aims his stick and makes a clean hit. The nine ball heads toward the pocket. I close my eyes.

He's got the shirt.

"Ohhhhhhhhhhh!" the crowd groans.

I open my eyes.

The Sledgehammer steps back shocked.

The nine ball's lying there hugging the cushion.

He missed!

I'm staring at the table.

"I believe it's your inning, Mickey V.," Big Earl says.

I step up to the table. It's me and the nine ball eyeballing each other. It's a two-rail bank of forty-five-degree angles. A maniac shot.

But to win, sometimes you've got to risk it all. I find my angle, sense the line shooting off the rail.

I aim the greatest pool stick in America and shoot. The nine slams once, twice, and zooms into the corner.

"That's the way!" Poppy screams.

I lift my stick in the air as everyone starts running toward me. My hand's killing me and I'm feeling fine.

Joseph runs over and hugs me and Mom is trying to punch through the screaming crowd.

Big Earl is pushing his way to me with the red shirt.

173

"It was a clean Vernon knockout!" Poppy says.

Big Earl is saying, "Mickey Vernon, I present you with the tournament shirt. You wear it proud."

I put it on; it's pretty big, but I can feel the pride pumping through me. The Sledgehammer comes up and shakes my hand.

"Congratulations, kid. Shirt wouldn't have fit me anyway."

"Thanks, Gordon. You played tough."

Arlen's waving his mechanical pencil in the air. Petie Pencastle and T. R. Dobbs plow through the big kids because this is a fifth-grade moment and should be shared by every ten-year-old in America.

"Fifth grade rules!" shouts T.R.

"All right now!" Poppy's trying to gain control.

The shouting and clapping die down. Snake Mensker starts it with his stick—pounding it on the floor in the pool player's applause. Joseph grabs a stick from the wall, the umpires follow, and one by one the players join in, pounding their sticks for me on the old gray tiled floor until the sound bounces off the paneled walls and echoes down from the ceiling.

It's the greatest honor a player can get. I'm hoping with all my heart that my dad can hear it in heaven.

I wear the red shirt for two weeks before I let Mom wash it. She says it stinks to high heaven and if she doesn't wash it soon, it's going to stand up by itself.

I only wear it to school once—the night of the science fair. My hand isn't hurting at all by then. Arlen and I hang Rory Magellan out to dry even though his mother lets him put the volcano in the middle of the big meeting room in Town Hall and everyone has to stand around while he gives a dumb speech about the importance of chemistry in our everyday lives that Arlen says would make Mr. Science heave. Rory pours Palmolive detergent into the volcano hole, adds some red food coloring, vinegar, and water. Then he quickly mixes baking soda with a little water and pours that in. If there's an eruption we all miss it. The volcano burps twice and one drop of reddish muck drips out. Sometimes chemistry in our everyday lives is a bust.

Rory's face is green, my favorite color, as Arlen slaps on his top hat and announces that Mickey Vernon, Vernon's Pool Hall Youth Tournament champion and soon to be nine-ball champion of the entire universe, is going to demonstrate our findings.

"Step up to the center ring," Arlen shouts, "and see the amazing secrets of the pool table."

Everybody does except Rory.

I perform death-defying shots on the little table that my dad and I learned to play on as kids while Arlen explains the math. I don't miss once.

Mayor Blonski tries a few shots and doesn't do as well as me.

Mrs. Riggles says she has never thought of a pool table as having "so many dimensions."

Arlen presents his chart, POOL IS ALSO ABOUT MATH, that he used to help me blow the Sledgehammer out of the water.

Lots of scrawny kids are interested in that one.

We win first prize.

The mayor shakes our hands and if he knows that Arlen's parents didn't vote for him, he isn't saying. He says we're "a credit to the town and the furtherance of science."

I let Arlen have the blue ribbon since I got the red shirt. Mrs. Pepper takes a picture of Arlen with all his science fair ribbons and Arlen sends it off to Mr. Science the next day.

I get my picture in *The Cruckston Comet* twice in one month.

Here's how the whole thing looks.

The Unbelievable Secrets of the Pool Table
by Arlen Pepper and Mickey Vernon
5th Grade Mrs. Riggles's Class
Grover Cleveland Elementary School

The Laws of the Universe are everywhere you look, even in places you wouldn't expect.

Isaac Newton's Laws of Motion
(at work on a pool Table)

1. Every body remains in a state of rest or uniform motion in a straight line unless acted on by forces from the outside.
(In pool talk this means a pool ball isn't going anywhere unless it's hit by something, and once it starts moving, it needs something to stop it, like a rail, another ball, or the friction of the cloth on the table.)

2. The amount of acceleration of a body is proportional to the actual force and inversely proportional to the mass of the body.
(The harder you hit a pool ball the faster it's going to move, and the less it weighs, the faster it will go.)

3. Every action has an equal and opposite reaction.
(A cue ball stops dead when it hits another ball straight on.)

Pool is also about Math!

"The universe stands continually open to our gaze, but it cannot be understood unless one first learns to comprehend the language and interpret the characters in which it is written. It is written in the language of mathematics, and its characters are triangles, circles, and other geometric figures, without which it is humanly impossible to understand a single word of it; without these, one is wandering about in a dark labyrinth."
—Galileo (1564-1642)

VECTORS FOR VICTORY
A vector is a line that takes you from one place to the next.

Some great pool players can picture vectors in their heads going from the balls to the pockets.

Bank Shots Use Geometric Angles

When you hit the eight ball at a certain angle to the rail, it will bounce off the rail at the same angle.

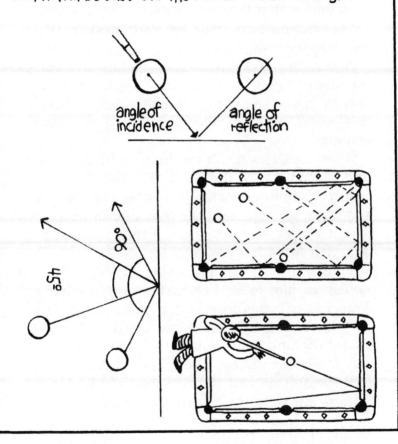

angle of incidence

angle of reflection

45°

90°

It's like my winning the tournament gets everything going.

Arlen and I win the jelly bean guessing contest at Pearlman's World of Fashion. We're only thirty-three beans off, which really impresses the store manager. She gives us a hundred-dollar gift certificate, but won't let us trade it in for cash, even when we mention that Pearlman's isn't a guy store.

"Maybe you boys could get your mothers a nice gift, hmmm?" she says.

Arlen convinces his mother to buy it from us for seventy cents on the dollar. "I ask you," Arlen says to her as she hands him the cash, "where in this world can you buy a hundred dollars for seventy?"

Arlen's parents finish the floor of his tree house and put up two of the sides. It's got a ways to go before it's finished. Arlen and I climb up there anyway while Mangler paws the tree and squeals. Arlen says it's a lesson to everyone living in this plastic age, that wood has power.

Francine starts talking to her father again and convinces him to let her have a dove for her act. Francine calls the dove Lester, which she feels was the deciding factor. Francine says that Lester will make her famous as soon as he learns to fly out of her magic hat without pooping in midair.

Buck isn't around much. I saw him by Vinnie's Variety last week, but when he saw me he looked away. I'm practicing pool twice a day except on Sunday because Poppy says even a world champion needs a day of rest. I'm setting my sights to play in the Northeast Youth Pool Open in Atlantic City in December. Joseph says he'll drive me there in the Peterbilt.

I can see why he and Dad were such good friends.

Joseph and Camille are becoming friends too. He tells her he can teach her pool, how to drive a truck, or how to make real Mexican enchiladas. Camille starts with a truck-driving lesson, but after that they both decide enchiladas are safer.

Joseph brings up buckets of barbecue from Texas (the best I've ever tasted) when Mom graduates from college. He and Mom understand each other more now, although it still really gets her when he talks "cowboy." Mom knows she can count on him; she says that's the biggest gift in friendship. We have a big party in Vernon's to celebrate Mom's graduation. Poppy hires Francine to do her magic act for the entertainment. Francine almost has a heart attack getting ready.

"Do you think I should wear my Easter dress or my stirrup pants and my sparkly tank top?"

Arlen and I look at each other.

"Do you think I should start with Lester coming out of the hat or work up to it and start with my flying scarves trick that I do to 'The Sound of Music'?"

"Well . . ."

"Your grandmother is a *saint*, Mickey. Do you know that?"

It's like the whole town comes to the party. Poppy, Camille, Serena, and I blow up a hundred balloons and hang them everywhere with ribbon. Francine starts with Lester; he flies out of her hat straight up to the ceiling fan and only comes down when she threatens to turn it on, but otherwise her show goes fine, even her card tricks. Everyone says it's only a matter of time before she plays Vegas. Francine walks through the rest of the party in her stirrup pants and sparkly tank top with a smile so happy it makes her braces glow.

Poppy and Big Earl sing songs from olden days while Big Earl plays his guitar. Mr. Kopchnik dances with Mrs. Cassetti. Camille kisses Brad Lunder by the Coke machine near the storage closet and Arlen gets a picture of it. Mom cries and says that having the party in the pool hall is perfect because she's learned so much living above it.

I know what she means. Every time I walk into Vernon's now I feel courage pumping through me. That's the thing about pool. Some people see numbered balls on a table and just learn the rules. But when the game's in your blood, you learn what's inside of you.